"I must go."

Kathryn could feel the tears welling in her eyes; she could not stay any longer and talk to Dalton as if she did not know him. She *did* know him— he was the only man she had ever loved. And she had left him…a gullible girl importuned by a dashing rogue. It had ruined her life. Now she was being touched by her past in a tangible way.

"Am I not to be granted the same privilege before you leave?" he asked gently. "As far as introductions go, this one falls sadly flat, but shall we blame our circumstances for the impropriety?"

His hair was a bit longer now; it hung a little over his collar. It suited him. *She had to stop this!*

Kathryn must flee and she knew it. She could spend no more time in his company and risk all she had worked for over the past four months. His strength and magnetism now scared her—she wanted to stay.

No! she screamed in her head.

"I cannot" was all she said.

Books by Mary Moore

Love Inspired Historical

The Aristocrat's Lady
Beauty in Disguise

MARY MOORE

has been writing historical fiction for more than fifteen years. After battling and beating breast cancer, Mary is even more excited about her career, as she incorporates some of her struggles throughout her books, dedicated to encouraging others in the Lord and using her writing for God's glory.

Her debut novel, *The Aristocrat's Lady,* won several acclaimed awards, including the 2011 Reviewers' Choice Award from *RT Book Reviews* for Best Love Inspired Historical, and the 2011 Holt Medallion from VRW for Best Book by a Virginia Author.

Mary is a native of the Washington, D.C., area, but she and her husband, Craig, now live in the beautiful Blue Ridge Mountains in southwestern Virginia. When not writing, she loves to read, minister in her church and spend time with her husband and black Lab, Darcy.

Mary would love to hear from you! She can be reached by visiting her website at www.marymooreauthor.com.

Beauty in Disguise

MARY MOORE

Love Inspired

Recycling programs
for this product may
not exist in your area.

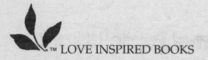 ™ LOVE INSPIRED BOOKS

ISBN-13: 978-0-373-82949-1

BEAUTY IN DISGUISE

Copyright © 2013 by Mary Moore

This edition published by arrangement with Love Inspired Books.

® and TM are trademarks of Love Inspired Books, used under license.
Trademarks indicated with ® are registered in the United States Patent
and Trademark Office, the Canadian Trade Marks Office and in other
countries.

www.LoveInspiredBooks.com

Printed in U.S.A.

And be kind to one another, tenderhearted, forgiving each other, just as God in Christ also has forgiven you.
— *Ephesians* 4:32

This book is dedicated to
Carol Taylor O'Leary

My Sister-In-Law
My Sister in Christ
My Very Dear Friend
Whom I Dearly Love!

Without her encouragement, support
and not-so-gentle persuasion
my writing career would still be
in a box in the attic,
and my heart might not belong to Jesus.

To God Be the Glory!

She walks in beauty, like the night
Of cloudless climes and starry skies;
And all that's best of dark and bright
Meet in her aspect and her eyes...

—*Lord Byron*

Chapter One

Sussex, 1814

"You!"

Kathryn had pulled her hood more closely around her face and turned to leave the bridge. What she ran into almost knocked the breath out of her. Two strong hands gripped her shoulders to steady her. When she looked up at the man towering over her, she spoke out of shock. It was *him*. Lord Dalton was here, and she almost said his name. She would have known him anywhere, even after nine years. He wasn't supposed to arrive until tomorrow. She was prepared for tomorrow, not for this.

"I beg your pardon?" he said, as he searched for her eyes in the shadows of her hood. "What did you say?"

"I…um…you…you frightened me." She was still shaky, though she knew complete safety in his grip.

"Steady there, waif. You have been too reflective this night. With your head in the heavens, you did not see me." He was smiling down at her, and she quickly pulled her hood even closer. Could it be possible he was even more handsome?

She must keep her wits about her. She must play the part. "Who are you?"

"Ah, I see it is to be direct interrogation from the start," he replied. "As a military man I recognize your tactics." His voice was deeper than she remembered, but she could not forget the playfulness always near the surface of his words.

Her voice had a quiet calm, and she followed her instinct to respond in playfulness. He always had such a wonderful sense of humor. Who would know? "Interrogation? With one question? Whose military were you a part of?"

He laughed out loud. "Touché, madam!"

"Could you please let me go? I am quite recovered." Why was he wandering around Trotton in the middle of the night? For that matter, why was he here a day early? And why hadn't he gone to the Manor? "What reason makes you wander about in the night?"

"I suspect my reason to be similar to yours," he said, grinning in the moonlight. "I could not sleep and decided the evening air might do the trick. As to my identity, my name is Dalton and I am presently staying at the inn in Midhurst."

Kathryn could feel the tears welling in her eyes; memories crashed in on her like the sea on the shore. She talked to him as if she did not know him. But she *did* know him—he was the only man she had ever loved. And she had left him…a gullible girl importuned by a dashing rogue. It had ruined her life. Now she was being touched by her past in a tangible way.

She could not turn back the hands of time, but could she make it stand still for this night?

"Am I not to be granted the same privilege?" he asked.

His hair was a little longer now; it hung over his collar. It suited him.

What was she doing? She could not risk all she had worked for over the past four months just because his strength and magnetism drew her in.

"Wait." The compelling but gentle hand still gripped her arms, holding her back. "You must not be afraid, lass, but I cannot let you go into the night alone. Please allow me to escort you to your home."

She kept her head down. She did not know if he would recognize her, but it was much more likely tonight, without her normal disguise, and that would ruin everything. He was getting a little too close.

"What are you about, Mr. Dalton? Let me go at once." She thought her deliberate ruse of dropping his title might be the only way she would have of throwing him off the scent, should he suspect. She tugged at the hand still gently holding her arm. "I am familiar with the landscape and I need no escort."

He scolded her seriously. "As you have proof before you, danger can lurk without your knowledge. I shall not let familiarity with the area sway me to leave a woman alone at midnight."

Kathryn did not struggle; she knew it would be futile. She only needed to await an opportunity to elude his grasp. But even now, she remembered the strength in those arms. They had once kept her close to his side when he had walked with her. They had once kept his famous horses in check while they drove to Richmond Park. And they had often held her safe while dancing to the strains of a waltz in a crowded ballroom.

She always thought him the handsomest man she had ever seen. She spent many a night, in her younger days, reliving the feeling of being in those arms during a waltz. But she was whisked from Town all too soon and tried to put that time behind her. And she had succeeded, until now.

Had she hurt him? It must have hurt him, even if he had not cared for her as much as she had cared for him. She had fallen under the spell of a well-known rake and believed his impassioned protestations of love. He was older and flattered her, and he made her elope with him.

No, to own the truth, she had agreed to that on her own.

She was too young to realize that the steady and truest love, Lord Dalton's love, was the only one worth having. And the price for that lesson was the loss of her reputation, her father's affections and God's presence in her life.

She stood thus, all the while knowing that the longer she stayed in close proximity to him, the more of a chance she took. But her feet seemed rooted to the spot. When told that he was coming to Dinsmore Manor, she had been shocked. In all of England, he was coming to the one spot she thought safe. And she remembered holding her breath, waiting, listening for the words *with his wife,* but they had not materialized. Now she did not know which was worse.

"Who are you?" he whispered. "Shall I awaken in the morning and this will all have been a dream? Only an illusion of my imagination destined to disappear?"

Tomorrow she *would* disappear just as he predicted, and he would see her no more. She would again don the disguise created to hide her true identity from the world, to protect her livelihood. He would never suspect that she was Lady Kathryn, the daughter of the Marquis de Montclaire, the young girl he had courted nine years ago in London.

She must not think about that. As long as her hood covered her face, could she not enjoy herself? Just for a few minutes.

"You make too much of a name, sir." She was still quiet and poised, but a little mischievous, as well. "Unlike you, I belong here. We are not destined to know each other, so there is no need for an introduction."

"It is as I suspected, then," he said, his voice deep and low. "You are an enchanted fairy. You know our future before it happens and predict pain for me if I am not to know you."

Despite the mesmerizing voice and the danger she feared, Kathryn did not falter. "I am no fairy. I only speak the truth."

"I know it cannot be, but…am I acquainted with you?" His words startled her. He *must* not learn her secret. He continued, "I do not believe in the bewitching tales of the Weald. You are flesh and blood and I am real. Where is the impediment to our meeting again?"

Kathryn soothed him with her voice. "Sir, it is after midnight in a moonlit glade. *Everything* will change with the daylight, as it always does. I will ask you again to please release me." She knew if she had not known who he was, she would have been terrified. She must act rationally, whether silly banter was involved or not!

"I fear once I release you, you will fly." He lifted her chin with one finger, but she did not look at him. His grip on her arm stayed any movement she intended. "I will not let you go under the threat of reality. Whether I escort you to your home or not, I demand an assurance—a token, if you will, that I have not dreamed this entire night."

"I have no such token," she said quietly, all too aware of what gentlemen usually wanted as a forfeit. At the same time, she knew he would never harm her.

"Since I have no scissors for a lock of your hair, I must exact my talisman from what is available to me." He lifted her hand to his lips for a gentle kiss. She remembered how amazing she felt the first time he had done so, even though nine years had passed. Her heart once again skipped a beat.

She made her body relax. The tension eased and they stood alone and silent, as she planned. "You now have your talisman. If you free me, I will not run away, but you must keep your distance."

She waited and he reluctantly released his grip on her, a reminder of the haven she had once known and had thrown away.

"I cannot remain, Mr. Dalton. I have already been here awhile."

"You promised you would not leave if I let go of your arm."

"So I did. However, *my* military training tells me I must say anything to obtain my freedom from an unknown assailant."

He chuckled again. "I think you know I will not harm you. Otherwise, you would have run the instant you *were* free."

"For some reason, I believe all thatchgallows say that to women who are alone in the middle of the night."

"Your instincts are sound. May I point out, however, that was I planning to pillage and plunder, I surely would have done so by now."

"Yes, but your army has already been found wanting once this night. And perhaps I should have warned you from the first—I am armed."

"Ah, yes, it is in the military codebook that if you are armed, you must so inform your assailant. May I ask with what are you armed?"

"If you knew my weapon, I would be at a complete disadvantage."

"You need not tell me. I have figured it out on my own. You are hiding a canon under your cloak. There, am I right?"

"My goodness, are you the last of your army?" He laughed again and she realized that even nine years later, she still missed his laugh.

"Who are you, my delight? Please give me your name and where I may call on you. I was extremely fearful this would be the dullest fortnight I have had to date. I believe you relieve me of my fear." He bent his head, trying to see her face beneath her hood.

"I am afraid I must go. It has been a pleasure to meet you, Mr. Dalton."

"Wait, give me your name, anything! When will I see you again?"

"I shall be elusive, and I shall be ever present."

"Say you will come again tomorrow night. This same time."

What was she doing? She was trying to recreate their past, only as more seasoned participants. She would be careful, she told herself. She would keep her cloak close around her. "Till tomorrow, then. Now I must go."

Turning, she ran as fast as her ragged breathing would allow. Afraid he would follow her, she ran straight for the small copse of trees, fading into its dark tentacles and finally stopping against one of Sussex's wide oaks to listen for the sound of his approach.

She stood quietly for several seconds trying to still her pounding heart, and soon grew confident that no footfalls or hoofbeats trailed her. After waiting a number of minutes, willing her breathing to slow, she turned toward the manor and began her walk back. She was overjoyed and saddened by an all-new taste of life she knew would never pass her way again. God had not forgiven her for her mistake. Why not add another to the list?

She would spend one more evening in his company, and then she would truly disappear.

Back in her room, she stared at herself in her tarnished mirror and it all came flooding back. As she lay down in her bed, tears rolled out of the corners of her eyes and dampened the pillow. Not only was she ruined beyond reparation and unwelcome in her own home, but she would be shunned should she seek help from any of her family or friends in London. No one would countermand her father's orders.

She had told Lord Dalton the truth. He would never see *her* again. Tomorrow she would don the trappings that grew more burdensome each day but made her unrecognizable to those in her previous circles. There had been no other option after she was abandoned by the rogue. She was alone and needed to make her own way in the world. But she could not do so as herself. She would disguise the beauty Lord Dalton saw tonight with the accoutrements of a dowdy wig, a pair of spectacles and lumbering shoes. Lady Kathryn would become clumsy and drab Miss Kate Montgomery, the hired companion of the daughter of the house.

And until tonight, that had been enough.

He came upon the bridge while allowing Merlin a drink of water, and he was mesmerized. It was uncanny. She reminded him of someone, though he could not think of whom. In the moonlight, he watched her pace up and down the bridge, assuming some kind of inner struggle, only to relax again and take in deep breaths of the night air. Her hood was farther back, and she had a beautiful profile in the light of the moon.

Dalton watched, bemused, as she ran from him. He knew any attempt to catch her up would be foiled by her own avowal of a deep knowledge of the terrain.

He stood solitary for several moments, a bit perplexed. What had come over him? He did not accost women he did not know. Perhaps *accost* was too strong a word, but something struck a chord with her. Was it her un-settled spirit? Her beauty? He hoped to find out at their next meeting.

He returned to the inn and lay awake a long time. It had been years since anyone had affected him so im-mediately…nine years, to be precise.

It had been his third Season and he'd only gone back to please his parents; *he* was ready for the army.

But he had met Kathryn—Lady Kathryn—and was very soon caught. She was young and in her first Sea-son, but she was so different from the usual debutantes that flooded London each spring.

She was beautiful, so beautiful she took his breath away. Would he ever forget those eyes? He feared not. They were sapphire-blue. And he could see into her very soul through them. Her raven hair was thick and luxurious and her skin creamy, with a little bronze from the sun. But even had she not been so beautiful, he be-lieved he still would have sought her out. She was self-less and intelligent. She smelled wonderful. They never tired of talking; they were so much in tune with each other's thoughts. And her heart belonged to God. They talked of Scripture for hours.

Many of his happiest memories were the ones when they had waltzed. It was the only time they were al-lowed to touch, and her touch was so calm and gentle. And in a dance, it was her gracefulness that swept him away. She floated in his arms, and he had begun to fall in love with her in only two short months.

And he had thought, at the time, that she felt the same. He need only wait for the proper time after speaking to her father. He would give up thoughts of the army and take up a profession that she would be proud of—one that would not keep them apart.

But she left him. He looked for her at every ball. He scanned the boxes for her at the opera. He would have set up camp on her doorstep, only the knocker had been removed and no one answered. He finally wrote to her father at Montgomery Hall, but received no response. He was only too happy then to buy his commission, and to this day, he carried a deep scar that kept him from trusting another woman completely.

Dalton repositioned his pillow, reminding himself yet again that the past was the past, and he must now marry and beget an heir.

He had been trained to judge the character of others quickly in his position as a major in Wellington's army. But in the Little Season he had only just left behind, he still doubted his ability to judge a woman. *She* had left him that curse.

And he knew not how he was to marry if he compared every woman to Kathryn. There had been no doubt in his mind that her feelings for him were as strong. He believed she, too, was falling in love. He had never misjudged someone so completely. It had not been so, and now he thought he could not marry for love. His heart was battered. He would wed based on credentials alone and pray that God would provide the companionship necessary to make the marriage work. He felt sure there was an eligible candidate, but he dreaded the search.

Heavenly Father, I know You will bring the woman You have for me in Your perfect timing. Please give me the patience to wait for her and for eyes centered on You to see her.

Yet before falling asleep, his last thoughts were of a waif in the moonlight, a winsome fairy who had taken his fancy.

"He will be here any moment. I demand you send Lacey elsewhere and help me complete my toilette!"

It was the next morning, and Kathryn heard Charity stomp her foot like a schoolgirl even though she could not actually see it. The talk had been of nothing but Lord Dalton for the past fortnight. She almost became sick of hearing his name until meeting him again last night on the bridge.

She had gone for one of her walks. She discovered after a few weeks in Trotton that could she shed her disguise even for an hour, she could bear the unwieldy trappings imposed on her by her own past actions. Once Charity was through with her for the evening, and usually only once a week, she would wait until the moon was high in the sky and take a solitary walk as herself.

She wore a voluminous cloak to cover her full appearance, but she had never really needed it until last night. She carried a small pistol her father had commissioned just for her. But no crime had come to the little town of Trotton for years, so she had not needed that, either. And she never saw another living soul at that time of night. Tales of goblins and trolls died hard in the Weald, and the Rother River Bridge was the source of many of those tales.

She was brought back to the present with another angry cry from Charity. "I believe you are not listening to me!"

Kathryn always tried to remain gentle and soft-spoken with her charge, but at times it was nearly impossible. "Charity, do *try* for a little decorum. No gentleman of fashion would arrive before noon." That was the truth, but she did not understand Lord Dalton's delay, as he was housed so close to the manor.

"You look quite nice in your apricot muslin, so I do not see how I may add anything to your appearance."

"Nice…nice…?" The young beauty before Kathryn balled her fists in a spoiled rage. "I think I look quite stunning in this gown!"

Kathryn heaved a sigh of resignation. "Charity, you must stop puffing yourself up. It does you no good and will surely put Lord Dalton off."

With her eyes closed in frustration, Kathryn wished she could get a message to Lord Dalton to flee for his life. She would not wish a fortnight of Charity upon him for any reason!

No, she must stop that line of thinking. She no longer knew him and had no right to determine what or whom he might like…despite their past.

She had desired nothing more than the darkness last night, a few moments of freedom. But today, despise it as she might, she was never more happy for the anonymity her masquerade brought her.

Her past mistake had haunted her for nine years, and she was no longer free to be Lady Kathryn. She was unwanted in London's elite world, and she must support herself now. She had learned years ago that it was only possible if Lady Kathryn disappeared and Miss Kate Montgomery took her place—a wig, a pair of spectacles and unwieldy shoes her only protection. She accepted her responsibility and the following consequences of her own mistake. She would not cry and complain of injustice; she would not grow into a bitter, angry woman. She accepted her punishment. She had made her bed, now she must lie in it.

She was presently in the nursery visiting with the younger members of the household. Charity's little sister chimed in, bringing Kathryn back to the present. "I am not vain, am I Miss Montgomery?" the child asked. She had adored Kathryn since the moment of her arrival, and it had become a mutual admiration very quickly.

Conversely, Charity had disdained Kathryn since the day she arrived. She flatly stated she had no need of a companion to teach her about the *ton,* and discarded Kathryn as she did all things for which she had no need.

Upon his return from London one month ago, Sir John Dinsmore, Charity's father, declared he had invited no less a personage than Lord Dalton to the manor. "Zounds, my dear, zounds," he had informed his wife. "The reputation of our stables has reached even to London! Even to London, upon my soul."

There had been little peace since.

She knew Sir John thought himself quite the strategist. Only four months ago, Lady Dinsmore had hired Kathryn as a companion to Charity. Her parents had finally accepted that as beautiful as their daughter might be, she had been spoiled for so long that they feared the girl's manners might hinder the possibility of an advantageous marriage. Even Lady Dinsmore could not be more excited. "Only think of it, Kate," said the lady when they were alone. "An unmarried earl under our roof for a fortnight. What a singular opportunity for our Charity!"

She spoke in a sterner voice to her daughter. "I am sure Miss Montgomery has mentioned that you must not seem too eager when the earl arrives. There is no doubt he will notice you straightaway, but he will wish to know you better should you behave the least bit… evasive."

Kathryn wondered if Lord Dalton's military training had prepared him for the challenge that awaited him in Charity Dinsmore! Even as she wondered how she would be able to bear the next fortnight. He would be in the same house; she would know he was near, but more than likely she would have no contact with him at all.

Why did the idea hurt so after all this time?

Chapter Two

Kathryn felt that she would never be able to concentrate today, but her practical heart had not failed her.

Sleep, however, had been another matter entirely, and had evaded her all night. Over and over again she relived Lord Dalton's words and actions. He held her as gently as a porcelain doll, but she was no less fettered. He spoke several times as if he could read her mind. And his kiss on her bare hand had been so very tender. To dwell on it again would only prolong the agony she thought had ended long ago. And yet she could not refuse him when he asked her to come again.

Thoughts of the past rushed through her mind. She had done the unthinkable—she had eloped. Almost from the time they could walk, young women were taught the importance of keeping a spotless reputation in the eyes of the *ton*. The two quickest ways to lose that invaluable status were simple: to be alone in the company of a single gentleman or to elope.

She was young and gullible and Lord Salford had

swept her off her feet. The feelings she'd had for Lord Dalton caused her to hesitate; how could her heart have changed so quickly? But Lord Salford knew what he was doing. He said that Lord Dalton had not complimented her enough. He had not demanded her company or declared her his only happiness. Lord Dalton was going to leave to go into the army and was only dallying with her affections. Looking back on it now, it was easy to see that Lord Dalton had been the truer gentleman, recognizing her youth and protecting her from the gossips.

But in the end it did not matter. Lord Salford said if he could not have her, he would die of a broken heart. Then he told her they must elope, as she was underage. Romantic thoughts disappeared. Indeed, she was horrified! She would be eighteen in a few months; why could they not wait until then? Why did he not go to her father and ask his permission? She was sure he would give it, though he might want her to wait those few months. No, Lord Salford said, her father would try to make her believe he was not good enough for her.

So they had traveled to Gretna Green to be married. She knew it was wrong; she wanted no part of it, but Lord Salford had been relentless and she was too young to see his actions as proof that he was not a gentleman. They spent four endless days on the road, only stopping to change horses and eat. The trip alone should have opened her eyes. Lord Salford had ridden alongside the coach for much of the time, and came inside at night to sleep. He was uncommunicative and sullen, offering none of the endearments he had generously doled out the previous few weeks. He feared her father would discover their intent and would follow them to stop the marriage. She was afraid to tell him she had left a note for her father explaining her actions. It would never occur to her to just disappear!

When they got to Scotland and Salford discovered that she did not come into possession of her fortune at eighteen, he left her. He never married her, and he abandoned her with only her pin money from last quarter. She found herself desolate in a strange country after traveling days in a carriage alone with Salford. She had done both of the things that would tarnish a young woman's name.

Her ruination had been complete.

Even her father could not forgive her, so he cast her off. And only a few short months later, Kathryn decided God could not forgive her, either. Life had become one unanswered prayer after another until she rarely sought Him anymore. She believed it made her stronger, but she missed the comfort and peace God had always given her.

Now she was to keep Charity in some semblance of proper behavior during Lord Dalton's visit.

"Oh, why does he not come? I am so bored I could scream. I should have accepted Harry Bolton's offer to go for a drive today. Now I am quite sorry I did not."

Kathryn sighed in frustration. "Charity, I am all out of patience with you. The past two weeks you have been anxious and overwrought. It will not bring him here sooner. I have told you again and again that a man of Lord Dalton's stamp will expect and *prefer* a properly behaved young woman, not one prone to go into a fit of the dismals."

Charity appeared to take her advice to heart as an hour later Kathryn sat in the window embrasure of the drawing room, as she always did during tea. Charity sat before the tea tray looking beautiful and demure. If only it had been natural and not by design.

Kathryn had gone to her room to freshen up, and once again sat in front of her mirror seeing a stranger. How she wished she could meet Lord Dalton without hiding behind her mask. It was impossible, of course, for many reasons. She knew he must despise her for what she had done to him. He would not be happy to see her. More importantly, she could not bear to see the pity on his face if he recognized her. She could avoid her previous life with her disguise. She could not bear it should he discover her identity and turn his back on her.

She came back to the present and watched young Lacey as she very slowly and meticulously carried an overfull cup of tea to her. "You are doing splendidly, sweetheart," she whispered. Lacey was starved for affection in the most pitiable way. She was sadly neglected, though Kathryn found her eager and willing to learn everything she could.

She was almost upon her with the cup of tea when the door opened and the butler announced in a deep baritone, "Sir John, Lord Dalton has called."

Kathryn's eyes sought the earl's face of their own volition, and she felt a nostalgic wish in her heart that it was she in Charity's place.

The teacup, so lovingly carried, rolled awkwardly

across the carpet and a horrified gasp was the only sound heard upon this stentorian announcement. Kathryn's quiet assurance directed at the disconcerted Lacey was the only thing that kept the self-conscious child from fleeing the room in tears.

"Jarvis frightened me, Miss Montgomery," whispered the dismayed little girl.

"Indeed he did, Lacey. It is of no matter, for we will clean it up momentarily." Kathryn discreetly bent to mop up part of the spill with her napkin as Sir John shifted his eyes from the small disaster to the man now coming toward him. Kathryn sensed Lord Dalton's awareness of the situation and appreciated that he did not draw even more attention to Lacey.

It made her remember his kindness. He was a more mature version of *her* Lord Dalton, but his characteristics appeared to be intact. She decided she could not be responsible for her wayward thoughts while he was with them.

"Dalton, my boy, welcome, welcome!" Sir John stepped forward in obvious exuberance, hand outstretched in greeting. "Told the ladies you and I had agreed upon no specific time of arrival, so we have begun tea as usual. Apologize profusely, my boy."

Lord Dalton entered the salon that seemed full of staring eyes. He realized that the two young children and one young girl were quite obviously Sir John's progeny. There was also a lady of indeterminate age sitting by the window, but based on her appearance she was not a guest.

His quick observations did not show in his expression. He greeted his host graciously in return. "Sir John, I am honored. Please feel no dismay over beginning your tea. More to the point, I must apologize to your lady for my late arrival. I had no wish to upset your schedule further, so as you see, I have presented myself in all my dirt. Do forgive me, please."

He could not tell them about this morning's pursuit. He had begun his search for the woman of last night at the inn and hoped to have her direction by noon. Though she said she would return tonight, he wished to be prepared. He wanted her name and where she lived. His old tendencies in the army died hard.

His efforts had been fruitless. Three hours later he had not uncovered one clue. The vacant expressions on the faces of the people he talked to were easily verified as truth and not an attempt to protect one of their own. Yes, he had seen her only by the light of the moon, but he was no young buck allowing romantic settings to invent what did not exist. Her beauty, though seen only in shadows, had been unmistakable even without a clear description of her features. But there had been the rub. He could give no one that description.

Such defeat only made him more determined. She would *not* disappear as Kathryn had. He would not allow it a second time.

She was a lady, of that he had no doubt. He might speculate on the reasons that brought her to the bridge in the middle of the night, but he was determined to find out why.

To own the truth, he chuckled at himself. Having

no luck finding her among the locals, he realized that her status as a lady might not be known to them. He decided he would question Sir John's household as to her name and whereabouts.

He also began second-guessing his leading from God. He was attracted to her and clearly felt he was to know her, an instinct telling him he might already know her, even while acknowledging that was impossible.

His mother had advised him to avail himself of Sir John's offer for a few weeks. He needed to accept what was due to his family name by finding a wife and setting up his nursery. But those he met during his short time in London seemed no more than schoolgirls only just out of their own nurseries! His mother suggested he stop trying to shop for a wife and let love come naturally.

He would not rest on his laurels as he could in Town. But women flocked to him in London, though he hated it. He need only pick one, yet not one had touched a chord in his heart. So he had taken his mother's advice to visit Sir John.

Here in Trotton, the delight he felt on the bridge when the fairy responded to his banter made him think that love might come naturally, after all. He would meet her tonight, then await an opportunity to know her in the daylight. He would try to overcome his fear that he would not be able to judge her character accurately.

His mind came back to the drawing room as Sir John greeted him in return. "Do not mention it, I say, do not mention it," he repeated in a now-familiar habit. "But you do remind me of my manners. Please allow me to introduce my family." He whispered an aside, "Not to worry that they'll be under your feet the entire visit, my boy, but I told them they must do the pretty to welcome you."

Dalton was led to a matronly woman, still possessing a good figure despite her cap and graying hair. She was introduced as Sir John's wife, but he had already deduced her parentage of the three younger members of the party. "My dear, this is Lord Dalton, who has come to put a few of my best hunters to the test."

Dalton bowed over the extended hand and smiled at the woman politely lowering her head in return. "Your servant, ma'am. I can only wonder at your generosity. My intention was to put up at the inn, but your husband would not hear of it. I vow to remain least in sight during my stay so as not to disrupt your normal routine."

"My lord," Lady Dinsmore said, chiding him, "you speak nonsense. Of course you will stay with us. I hope you will find it quite comfortable here. Being so far from London, we are always exceedingly happy to have company."

She arose and began to walk toward the fireplace. She continued speaking, and it was obvious that she expected him to follow. "Indeed, we stand upon no ceremony here."

It was then that Dalton became conscious of the young lady seated on the settee before the fire to which Lady Dinsmore had been leading him. His heart knew a moment's hope that the woman he met last night sat before him, but immediately he deduced that the blond child bore little resemblance to his midnight wanderer.

"Before we overwhelm you with the entire family, I will introduce you to my daughter so that you may receive your tea and make yourself more comfortable. I fear you must be fainting from malnutrition."

Standing six feet two inches in his stockings, his size belied her statement so shockingly that he began to laugh, feeling that he might enjoy a stay with such a family.

He was once again aware of the woman in the window embrasure. Her lowered head shot up at his laughter.

Lady Dinsmore led him to the young woman serving tea, who flushed prettily and slowly raised large eyes of deep green. She was exquisite, but she was merely a child, and he had no interest in schooling his wife!

"This is my oldest daughter, Charity, my lord. She has been eager to meet such a distinguished guest," she said, and with a maternal pat on his arm, added, "and to hear all about London. I am afraid you will be heartily sick of relating the latest *on dits.*"

The *very* young lady bowed her head in greeting. He thought no further than proper manners in meeting the child.

So when he bowed low in turn and again smiled at the girl, it was with the same courtesy as he used to greet her father. "Miss Charity, I am charmed, I'm sure. I understand this is where I am most likely to receive a cup of tea," he said, smiling. "So beautiful a young lady goes a long way to reviving one. However, I confess that a cup of tea would not come amiss."

"Oh, my lord, how kind," the girl said, batting her

eyelashes at him brazenly. He was honestly at a loss for words at her behavior, but he was able to mutter a quick thank-you when she handed him his cup.

Dalton heard a weary sigh from the woman in the window seat. Apparently, she was also aware of the young girl's impropriety. Indeed, her parents did not seem to notice. He decided then and there that he wished very much to meet the woman who was so quiet, but all-observant.

Kathryn covertly watched the events unfold in front of her from the moment he walked into the room. His charm completely won over his hosts. His manners were impeccable, and his smile was heart-stopping, releasing the two dimples she had never been able to get enough of in London. They had been well hidden in the shadows of the night before, though she could not remember whether he had actually smiled at her or not. She was glad for her out-of-the-way placement and the opportunity it afforded to watch him openly without attention.

She was wrenched from her ruminations as Lady Dinsmore signaled for Jacob.

"My lord," she began, "I should like you to meet my two youngest." Jacob bounced off his chair as Lacey left Kathryn's side, and both joined their mother.

"Lord Dalton, I should like to make you acquainted with my son and daughter, Jacob and Lacey."

All watched as Jacob put one arm across his stomach and one arm behind his back and bowed deeply from the waist. The room smiled as a whole, excepting his older sibling, as he made his first attempt at being a young gentleman. Jacob was eight and showed not the slightest tendency toward the Dinsmore handsomeness. But Kathryn had grown to love the young boy, who was grateful for someone's attention and, though a little boisterous, for the most part just wanted to be loved.

Lacey, more prone to shyness, curtsied very prettily with downcast eyes and muttered politely, "We are pleased you have come to visit us."

Lord Dalton did not disappoint. Bowing very deeply himself, he lightly grabbed the hand of the little boy and shook it quite fashionably. "Your servant, Master Jacob. I look forward to your advice on the horses, as well. I am sure I can count on your judgment."

Jacob's eyes widened to twice their normal size, and he looked over his shoulder at her and giggled.

Lacey, in the meantime, was having her small hand kissed by the dashing lord bent on one knee before her. His eyes, quite level with hers, twinkled as he released her hand and said, "I can see that Trotton must feel very graced indeed at having two such beautiful sisters in their midst."

Lacey could only stare, her mouth agape, but as he rose to his full height, she turned to her with a smile, as dazzling as any Charity could muster. Kathryn was a little embarrassed to feel tears form in her eyes at the happiness of the two little ones and felt completely unnerved to be so proud of a man she had absolutely no right to be proud of. She felt the tug of her heartstrings. That heart, the one she thought long ago on the shelf, was beating erratically and she sighed inwardly.

Kathryn's mind was stayed on Lord Dalton. How

she wished she could meet him as herself as she had last night under the cover of darkness. Would he turn away from her, as well? She had no reason to believe he would not. She had only the actions of other men to judge since her fatal mistake. Despite his manners, he would no doubt feel the same.

So lost in her thoughts was she that Lady Dinsmore's voice barely broke through before she realized they were coming toward her. Kathryn stood, determined not to fear detection, and curtsied with a lowered head as he bowed to her in turn. She seemed to hear their voices from very far away.

"My lord, Miss Montgomery is Charity's companion. We are so fortunate to have her to teach Charity the ways of the *ton*. We would not want it said our girl did not have proper manners."

"Miss Montgomery, I am happy to make your acquaintance. I can see that though these little ones are not in your charge, they clearly show their devotion to you. Miss Charity must share you, it seems." How had he guessed that? Ah, that intuitiveness—he always knew what she needed before she knew herself.

His smile disarmed her, and the dimples alone caused her heart to race. "Thank you, my lord," she said.

She was surprised that he remained by her side.

"Have you been in London recently, Miss Montgomery? I admit to only a short stay before coming here, but I do not recall seeing you there."

Kathryn was not prepared for this discourse. She never thought to have conversation with him so soon, if at all. She had no time to put on the mantle of servitude she had contemplated when she knew he was coming. "No, my lord, I have not been to London for many years, thank you for asking."

"I do not know the precise time you were there, but I, too, have been away from it for some time, and I do not find it changed in the least."

Should she betray what she knew? "Of course. I believe Sir John mentioned that you had been in the army."

"That is true. However, in addition I have been the past four years learning to run our family estate. My brother was killed in a hunting accident, and I had to sell out and return home." She could tell the hurt was still raw, and she wanted to comfort him. He quickly smiled. "Perhaps we met in London many years ago?"

"I do not believe so, my lord." She looked at him, knowing her spectacles hid the mischief in her eyes. "My Season was cut short, but perhaps you have guessed that I did not…take?"

She slowly smiled, letting him know the joke was on her, but he surprised her with his own grin, dimples becoming quite evident. "Ah, then you were the one! Every other debutante I met while in London had more hair than wit! I seem to remember hearing of the woman with such a gift for conversation that she was a must at every gathering."

She could not help herself, and laughed outright. He had been so charming to everyone he met, she still could not be completely sure he was not being the perfect gentleman, but she surmised he was laughing with her in return. For one instant her heart was lighter than it had been in years, but it grew heavy again as she remembered what she had lost. The thought of it made her smile disappear.

"Forgive me, Miss Montgomery, I have let my sense of the ridiculous get the better of me. I thought…"

"No, no, my lord. You said nothing amiss. I have only remembered something that I…"

"*Kate!* What can you be about?" Charity's patience had run out. Oh, dear, what was she doing? She moved aside as Charity put her hand on Lord Dalton's arm. "You must wonder at us, my lord," she spoke in a conspiratorial voice. "I have never sanctioned having Kate present at tea, and now Mama will have to agree with me. I apologize for her lapse in judgment in monopolizing the conversation."

"I quite disagree, Miss Charity. Miss Montgomery and I were just exchanging pleasantries. I believe you must be well satisfied in your mother's choice of companion for you."

No, Lord Dalton had not changed. Kathryn knew she must leave his presence. "Lady Dinsmore, shall I take the children to the nursery so you may visit with your guest?"

"Yes, yes, do let them go." She heard Charity sigh as she left. "I am sure you must wonder at us, my lord, but Mother *will* have them to tea with the adults."

Kathryn heard the low timbre of Lord Dalton's voice descry her annoyance. He told her he had been charmed and had several nieces and nephews he enjoyed very much when he visited his sister at Michaelmas. She was once again pleased that he did not hide his joy for children, as many men would have. Indeed, she was too pleased with everything about him!

Would she be able to keep her countenance when around him? Her heart had betrayed her the night before, and she felt it again in the drawing room only moments ago. She knew it would be a tough battle to overcome her renewed feelings, but it was one she *must* win. To use his vernacular, she would need the entire arsenal to make it happen.

Chapter Three

Kathryn felt the need for air. Charity was no doubt resting before getting dressed for the evening, so she took a walk down to the lake the children loved so much.

She needed to gain her composure.

After the debacle in Scotland, Kathryn had run to the only person left in her life she could trust. Dear Miss Mattingly! Her old governess folded her in her arms and let her cry for all she had lost. She alone had offered comfort and forgiveness to a vulnerable young woman. Matty had taught her to be the open and honest woman she had grown to be. Dear Miss Matty had been a living Bible to Kathryn; she lived it every day of her life, and Kathryn believed it by watching her.

Matty wanted her to go back to her father, but Kathryn could not. He had made it plain that she was no longer part of his life.

After years of Kathryn being at the mercy of jealous wives and gentlemen who thought she was fair game, Matty had created the mask that made Kathryn feel safe enough to go on with her life. Matty believed God had helped them make a plan out of dire need, so she felt thankful, not guilty.

Now, sitting on the bench overlooking the lake, she bent to rub her ankles where her odd shoes rubbed against them. She was thankful that they had finally been broken in enough to prevent the blisters and pinching they had caused at first.

Matty had warned her that her natural poise could be her undoing. So she had found the most cumbersome and unwieldy pair of shoes imaginable. They not only made her poor feet very sore, they gave her a perfectly awkward gait and an age-defying shuffle.

Matty had then insisted on her spectacles. The blue tint hid the eyes that had inspired insipid poetry and gawking stares since she was sixteen years old. Matty said her eyes could ruin her facade in seconds. So they decided that covering them was paramount. She was aware that she could easily knock her spectacles askew or accidentally drop them, destroying all of the anonymity she worked so hard to achieve. But they determined if the shade were similar to the actual blue of her eyes, it allowed her to plant the slightest doubt in the mind of anyone who might witness such a mishap. She would prefer not having to wear the offending articles at all, but they served their purpose.

Kathryn's final attempt at becoming a nonentity involved her hair. She could not cut it off. She knew it was her one act of defiance against the consequences of her situation and, therefore, had kept it, determined to find some other way to disguise it.

That was when Matty had the idea for her horrid brown wig. It was long and quite poorly made, but when she put it on her head and attached it tightly to her own hair, she was able to pull it all into a chignon that anchored it at her nape.

With that, her disguise was complete.

Now Lord Dalton was here, and the first meeting was over. He was so much the same and so much changed that he was able to surprise her out of countenance. But she was better prepared now and would no doubt see little of him during the remainder of his stay.

Therefore, it was quite a shock when she passed by the stables on her way back to the house and ran into him coming toward her.

"Miss Montgomery, this is a pleasant surprise." He bowed then smiled.

"My lord!" she said, and curtsied. So much for only seeing him at tea! "Charity had no need of me, so I took a walk down to the lake."

"*I* thought to get my first look at some of the horses, but could not locate Sir John."

"I will be happy to send a servant to bring him to you." She curtsied again and turned to go. His hand stayed her, and she looked up at him in surprise.

He laughed, and her brow furrowed in question, though it did not stop her from admiring his brown eyes. "You are too efficient, ma'am! I do not wish to disturb him, and I can easily look them over without him." He surprised her again. "Will you join me?"

"You are too kind, my lord, but I will leave you to your inspections."

"On the contrary, I would appreciate the company, and you know your way around better than I." She started to speak again, and he cut her off with mischief in his eyes. "You *did* say Miss Charity had no need of you."

She finally laughed as he intended. "You are quite persuasive, sir."

"And 'you cannot refuse a request from a guest' is all that is needed to make me feel a complete cad!"

She did not realize how she had forgotten his wonderful banter. "Oh, no, I am not paid to entertain the guests!" He looked at her askance, and when she smiled, they both burst out laughing. Drat the man! How could he turn her back into a seventeen-year-old so easily? She must watch her step.

"I pronounce the penalty for your levity—you must accompany me with no more excuses."

She began to lead the way. "Of course, my lord. I did not mean for you to think I did not *wish* to accompany you."

"Splendid. I saw a beautiful chestnut down a few stalls when Merlin was taken in. I believe it is along the row to the right."

"Merlin? What an excellent name for a horse. Is he a magician, then?"

"Absolutely, Miss Montgomery. He is fearless, as well. He carried me through many a battle I might not have survived without him. He is a great goer."

"What an important thing about war I have just

learned." She was quite serious. "I think, as females, we are believed to need shielding from actual details of battle. I wish it were not so." She came back to the present. "Of course, your mount would become your partner of sorts."

"You are quite right, Miss Montgomery. Are you a rider yourself?"

Kathryn was thrust back in time, when her father taught her to ride astride in breeches, her hair tied back with only a ribbon. "I used to, my lord, but it has been many years now. I had such a wonderful horse. We grew to trust each other implicitly."

"I do believe you actually understand. I have never heard it described quite like that, but that is exactly the word—*trust*."

What in the world was she doing? How would a lowly companion know such things? Thank goodness she had not told him her horse's name. With her luck he would have remembered it!

"Is this the chestnut you mentioned?"

"Yes, it is. She's a beauty, in truth." He went to the horse's head to rub her jaw. The horse let Lord Dalton know she did not appreciate him taking liberties with her by pawing the ground and shaking her magnificent head. He slowly reached into his pocket and drew out a palm full of sugar cubes. He put them near enough for her to smell. She danced around the stall and blew great breaths out of her nose, her way of informing him she was not so easily bought, but while he never moved his hand, she slowly drew in closer. As she took the treats from him, she let him slide his hands down her neck and under her mane.

Kathryn began to laugh. He looked at her, as if believing she would soon share with him what was so amusing. "I am sorry, my lord," she said, trying to catch her breath. "She is called Jezebel because she wants to control the men who come around her. Sir John will be devastated to know his Jezebel can be bought by a handsome man bearing sugar cubes!"

He laughed outright. "I get the feeling it is you and not Sir John who would love to see me bested by this beauty. Make no mistake, she will definitely be given the opportunity to try."

"I shall be sorry to miss it! I am afraid I must go, my lord. No doubt Charity will soon be looking for me." She was surprised when he once again stroked the horse and then turned to walk back with her.

"I have noticed that Miss Charity does not seem to get on with the younger children. Is it the age difference between them?"

Kathryn would have loved to warn him that Charity does not "get on with" anyone, but she would not so malign anyone in this family. "The age difference is quite a barrier, to be sure. I wish it were not so, because Lacey is at the age where she needs someone older to emulate, but I do not think it will be Charity at this phase in Charity's life."

"It appears to me that Lacey wishes to emulate you."

"Me!" She laughed at him. "She needs to be loved, and that she gets from me, but I am not the role model for her, either."

"I think you underestimate your relationship, but you know better than I. It is clear she seeks your approval, and you give it quite freely. A perfect companion."

She laughed at him again. "And therein lies the rub. I am not *Lacey's* companion!"

She had enjoyed herself immensely, but she must not get too close. She would never doubt his intense study of others or his well-honed instincts. She turned the conversation back to him. "My lord, I was very sorry to hear about the death of your brother." He turned to her and stopped walking, looking at her oddly. She stopped, as well. "You mentioned it at tea as the reason you had to leave the army." He relaxed, and she realized he wondered how she had known that. She had read it in the newspaper, but she never would have mentioned it had he not done so already. She definitely needed to heed her instincts and stay away from him and his personal life. "I can only imagine that the loss, along with having to completely uproot your life, must have been a great burden." No, she did not need to imagine; she understood it all too well.

"I thank you, Miss Montgomery. It certainly changed my life, but I am…content for the moment. My mother is at home, and I am glad to be with her. She is a blessing to me in many ways, but especially in dealing with our tenants. She was adamant that she could take care of things and that I should go to London."

"She sounds like the perfect mother!" Kathryn had loved to listen to him talk about her when they were together so many years ago. "You did not wish to go?"

He hesitated. "I confess I am much happier in the

country. But she wished me to...enjoy myself after the years of learning to manage the estate." Kathryn knew that is not what he meant to say, but they had reached the house and she thought it was a good time to distance herself from him.

"Good afternoon, my lord. I hope you enjoy your stay here."

"Thank *you,* Miss Montgomery. I believe I will."

Dalton liked her. He thought he would when they had conversed at tea. And he had been right. She was serene, but her sense of the ridiculous seemed always hovering, very near the surface in her conversation. She was easy to talk to and quick to laugh. And how her appearance changed when she did! He wondered at thinking her stodgy and middle-aged upon first seeing her in the window embrasure!

He had waited patiently to be presented to the woman with her hair so severe and who so obviously occupied the position, he now knew, of companion to the spoiled daughter. They had shared a few moments of banter, and he determined he might wish to spend as much time with *her* over the next two weeks as with any other member of the Dinsmore family. In fact, there were two things that greatly piqued his interest in the woman.

First, her odd spectacles. They were tinted, not *that* unusual, but they were of a dark blue shade and kept her eyes completely hidden. Perhaps she had some malady in which light or any brightness caused her pain. He *had* heard of such. But he was an excellent judge of character, and that came from reading others' eyes. He thought it might be interesting to learn more of her difficulty, though she had a well-honed sense of humor. *He* had a well-developed need to discern the characters of the people around him. It became a small challenge to talk to her in the dim light of the evening when she would, he hoped, not need to wear the offending glasses.

But even without seeing her eyes, he was quick to notice the two children turn to share their surprise and joy with Miss Montgomery, not their sister, not even their mother! After Lady Dinsmore introduced him and before she gathered the children, he determined that he would know her better. In his experience, the trust of a child went a long way in showing a caring character. She appeared to be the one person in the house who had shown genuine, honest emotion.

He could not put his finger on it, but there was also some mystery there. He doubted he would get the time to figure it out within the fortnight, but that she was obviously a lady fallen on hard times was the least of it.

His intent had been to get Merlin and go back to Midhurst. He thought he could spend the afternoon in search of information about the woman he met on the bridge the night before. He was not disappointed, however, by spending the time with Miss Montgomery.

Had it been Miss Charity he stumbled upon, he would have been frustrated indeed! The chit seemed intent on flirting with him and leaning on his arm since he arrived. She was beautiful; there was no denying that. But beauty without intelligence and kindness could not keep his interest. Only look at how he preferred Miss Montgomery.

He supposed the girl would do well enough when she came out; she probably had a respectable dowry attached to her person, but she had been positively brazen with him and she could be no more than seventeen. Normally, he would steer clear of such a child, but staying here put them in close quarters. Worse, still, was that her parents did nothing to stop her forwardness. He was beginning to believe Miss Montgomery could be his only ally in the house. Miss Montgomery and Jezebel, that is!

To Kathryn, the rest of the day passed slowly, she knew why. It was because she was to meet Lord Dalton again tonight on the bridge. One minute she was excited at the thought of spending time with him alone; the next, she berated herself for taking such chances, risking exposure. She told herself she would not agree to go again. This had been a mistake, and she seemed prone to them. But she would keep her promise to meet him this night, and then the cloaked woman would disappear.

She ate little dinner; she was too nervous. She did every possible thing wrong while helping Charity retire for the night. "He did not come to the drawing room after dinner! I am so vexed. How am I supposed to make him fall in love with me if I am never to see him?"

"Charity, he was probably tired after his trip." What a bouncer! He had been in Midhurst since the previous night. "You must prepare yourself. He is here to buy horses, and that will be his primary purpose each day. Everyone other than your father will have to play second fiddle to the horses."

"Pshaw!" she said, asking Kathryn to stop brushing her hair with such force. "I will make him so besotted with me that horses will fall to the wayside. You see if I don't."

"I wish you the best of luck."

"You know, Kate, you *can* be fired. You may have Mother bamboozled with your talk of London. But I have Papa in my pocket. I would watch your step if you wish to remain here."

She finally went to bed and Kathryn went to her room, dressed in one of her oldest walking dresses, and waited, sitting on her bed until the house was quiet.

The grandfather clock struck eleven-thirty.

She went out of the back of the house. Heaven forbid they should run into each other leaving the manor!

When she arrived, he was already waiting, but not on the bridge. He was with Merlin, leaning up against a tree, cheroot in hand.

He had not yet seen her, and she began to have second thoughts. What was she doing? Last night and today she had concluded there was no harm in this midnight madness. Suddenly, she wondered what good could come of it. One night of reliving the past was not enough reason to risk her life here in Trotton. And meeting with a man clandestinely was still wrong, though she was already ruined.

Had she learned nothing in nine years?

"Will you not come the rest of the way?" His voice startled her. Did he know she was there all along?

She stepped out of the shadows and walked up to Merlin. "May I touch him, my…Mr. Dalton?"

"I do not think he will let you, ma'am. Once trained for the army, they know not to let the enemy steal them away. But they have no idea who the enemy is, so they must learn only to trust their masters."

Even as he finished the last, Merlin turned his nose to her shoulder, almost knocking her down. Lord Dalton was at her side in an instant.

"I am fine, sir. I do not think he meant me harm. He just caught me off guard." To prove her point, she began to whisper softly to him, remembering not to use his name yet. Though she had learned that name in the afternoon as Miss Montgomery. He would have caught that lapse in a moment.

She put one hand on his neck, rubbing the taut muscles under his mane. She placed the other on his nose.

"How wonderful it is to be made a fool of by your own horse. But I am impressed, fairy. Perhaps you are kindred spirits. Merlin senses you are not of this world."

"Ah, Merlin," she cooed to the horse. "I knew there was something magical about you." He used his front hoof to paw the ground. She laughed, and it felt good. Too good.

"May we go to the bridge, sir? I am not comfortable here in the shadows."

He dropped his cigar, stepping on it as he followed her. "I got the impression you were not comfortable at all."

"Not uncomfortable, only aware that this was not a good idea." She held on to her hood at the breeze blowing across the river. "I realized what you must think of me and was going to leave."

"I think you are a lonely woman who enjoyed my company. Not lonely, perhaps, more sad."

"A mind reader! Do you tell fortunes, as well?"

"It did not take a mind reader to see that you were troubled last night. You paced, then calmed, then paced again. And yes, I do tell fortunes. I predict that your sadness will change when you meet a stranger on a bridge."

She laughed spontaneously.

"You see?"

"I have not so much as a ha'penny with which to pay you."

"Very well. In recompense, you must tell me your name."

"Did we not chase that rabbit last night?"

"Yes, but I did not catch it."

"You, Mr. Dalton, are very tenacious. But I cannot give it to you. I am sorry." She noticed he never corrected her when she called him mister. She wondered why. Surely a woman who would agree to such a meeting would be more forthcoming to an earl.

"And am I not to see your face?"

"No, sir."

"May I ask why?"

"I think not, it is a very long story," she said. "No doubt you will think me married and having a flirtation behind my husband's back?"

"It is one of many reasons why it could be so, but I did not think it of you."

"I must go. I am sorry to have agreed to this, but it is very wrong." She pulled her cape closer around her and began to move away.

"I only wish to talk." His voice was quiet. "You see, I am a little sad myself today."

Her sympathetic heart heard his, and she did not know what to do. Oh, how she had loved him. Would that she could take him in her arms and comfort him. Instead, she decided she would make him laugh.

"You know, I am not really a fairy. The truth is…I have never told anyone this, but I am in fact the troll that lives under the bridge."

His head came around slowly, unprepared for what she was saying.

"Shh! You see, a wicked ogre placed a spell on me and I can only be myself when the moon is full. In the dark and during the day, I am doomed to scare little children." She looked both ways then whispered, "Do you think Merlin has a spell to release me?"

Merlin's master let out a laugh that was music to her ears.

"How unfeeling! I think I would rather talk to him, anyway." She turned her nose up, though still buried in the cloak, and began to walk past him.

"No, no," he said, laughter in his voice. "You must have human company on this moonlit night."

"Well, that is what I thought, but you laughed at my secret!"

"So sorry," he mumbled.

They were both comfortable to be quiet for a moment and enjoy the night.

"Do trolls get married?"

She choked, remembering he, too, had a sense of humor.

"Oh, dear, I do not know! I am sure one has never been asked, though." She leaned back against the bridge. "I suppose it would only be wise to drop by during the day to visit the troll half. When I am the troll, I am not this charming."

"Or I could come on a moonless night."

"Yes, I suppose you could do that, but you would not get a good look at me then, and that really would be important to know before asking me to marry you."

"Oh, did you think I meant you? I am so sorry. There is a troll I've had my eye on in Rye! I have been too shy to ask. Please forgive me."

At that, they both laughed, and it echoed through the trees and across the water. As they wiped the tears streaming down their faces, he turned serious. "Will you please tell me who you are so I may call on you?"

She was ready for the quick change in subject.

"I am sorry, sir. I cannot. The reasons are too complicated to overcome, and I only came tonight because I could not bear to think of you waiting here." She put her hand on his face. "This is goodbye, Mr. Dalton. But thank you for curing my sadness. Thank you for everything."

With that, she ran off again and he did not follow her.

Chapter Four

"But I cannot, Lady Dinsmore!" Kathryn exclaimed, horrified. "It would be most unseemly!"

"Mother, I absolutely refuse to consider it. Why, I should be mortified!"

"Charity, you will hold your tongue. This is between Miss Montgomery and me."

The three ladies were in the sewing room, and Lady Dinsmore had become quite adamant. "Kate, last night's dinner was a disaster. Sir John and the rector said only ten words between them, and Charity," she said, giving the girl an evil glance, "did nothing but throw herself at Lord Dalton. He showed himself quite at ease with you during tea yesterday. I believe he will enjoy his meals more could he share them with someone who had London in common. Besides, it will solve the problem of uneven numbers, as well. I meant to mention the matter to you last week when I invited Mr. Wimpole to dinner during Lord Dalton's stay, but I confess it quite slipped my mind."

"I can assure you, my lady," Kathryn argued in an agitated manner, "Lord Dalton will be much more shocked to find himself seated at the table with a companion than he would be to see uneven numbers!"

"Oh, Mama, it does not bear thinking on. You always say we must defer to Kate's opinion regarding the activities of the *ton*. He will consider us…rustics!" The last was said with such horror that Kathryn could barely stop herself from laughing.

Lady Dinsmore had not expected such a to-do, and she began to be vexed. "Miss Montgomery, I am perfectly aware how to run my household despite your considerable knowledge of Society's dictates."

Kathryn had the grace to blush. "My lady, I certainly never meant…"

"Of course you did not, my dear. I know in London it might seem a little out of the ordinary, but we are not in London. And you know I quite consider you part of the family."

"Lady Dinsmore, please, I should be most uncomfortable. You can use the country as an excuse for the odd count or the informality. Pray, do not ask me to socialize with your guests."

The good lady sat rigid and quiet for a moment. "Well, I certainly never thought to hear you refuse a request for help, Kate. I was obviously quite mistaken in you."

Kathryn knew she was being manipulated, just as she knew the entire house was being manipulated in order to make Charity shine. But she was torn between what she owed Lady Dinsmore and her mixed emotions about Lord Dalton.

And that was the crux of the matter. Kathryn knew if it were anyone else in the world, she would not have been so adamant in her refusals. She must not let him have so much power over her, especially after last night. It would be too easy to fall in love with him again. He had changed only for the better, so how could she not?

"Oh, Lord Dalton, I have ever so many friends I should like you to meet." The child had not stopped talking since they sat down. Dinner the previous night had been interminable. The gentlemen said little, and Lady Dinsmore obviously had no control over her forward daughter. Miss Montgomery was not even in attendance.

He determined to find some excuse from dinner during most of his stay, but knew he could not do so after the dismal experience of last night. His hostess was astute enough to know why.

He was brought back to the present as Charity droned on. "Of course, they are not as fashionable as you and I are, but they enjoy my company." Why did Lady Dinsmore not stop her daughter from touching his arm and shoulder each time she made a comment?

The doors to the dining room opened, and Dalton was never so happy to see anyone as he was to see Miss Montgomery shuffling into the dining room. Another entire dinner with the vain, loquacious daughter of the house would make him wish to impale himself with his fork! The companion quietly apologized for not joining them in the drawing room before dinner, and slowly lowered herself into the vacant chair diagonal to him.

When Dalton stood upon the entrance of Miss Montgomery, he knew they could not have such discourse as they had enjoyed yesterday in the stables, but he certainly hoped for a rational conversationalist unlike the singularly quiet males and the inane females he presently enjoyed. If Miss Montgomery failed him, he would make up his first excuse for tomorrow evening.

He noticed the dignified lady's blush as he stood. Sir John remained occupied with his plate, completely ignoring a gentleman's duty, while the rector's attention was so focused on food, he apparently did not even hear her enter. Intuitively, though, he knew she was embarrassed at *his* gesture, not their lack of one.

She waved him to his seat with a quick hand. Interrupted from his turbot, Sir John responded with surprise to Miss Montgomery's presence. "Ah, joining us for dinner, are you? Excellent, excellent."

Did she not normally dine with the family? He gave Lady Dinsmore more credit than he had previously accorded her. She knew exactly what he felt last night, and she knew exactly how to remedy it. He should have guessed that Charity's companion did not dine with the family despite being in attendance at tea. He wondered if the beauty beside him was not a little petulant because of it.

"I am sure Mama would have accepted your excuses were she aware that your schedule did not fit in with ours," she said, the sarcasm dripping from her lips.

At such a small and intimate gathering, Dalton's one solace was being allowed to converse with the entire group rather than confined in the normal way to only those on his immediate left and right. "Miss Charity," he chided, trying to dampen her pretension yet preserve his manners, "I beg of you, do not make Miss Montgomery more uncomfortable than she no doubt already is. I daresay she was caught up with something of importance and there was no intent on her part to slight us." He smiled most charmingly.

He received a smile of thanks from the plainly dressed woman, and he regretted that she did indeed wear her spectacles at night. When she smiled, he noticed her even white teeth and rather high cheekbones. But he had a feeling that her eyes spoke more thanks than her expression. And he knew an earnest desire to please her. It was quite odd! Who would have anticipated he would experience the mystery of two completely different women when he accepted this invitation?

Lady Dinsmore chimed in as she was wont to do after the spoiled belle put her dainty slipper in her mouth. He did not envy her parents having to fire off the girl beside him. Why, she was as volatile as Prinny himself!

"Charity, Miss Montgomery *did* mention she would be a few minutes late this evening." Lady Dinsmore smiled at him. "Apparently, Jacob is planning a surprise for your lordship."

"Perhaps we should ask Miss Montgomery to tell us of young Jacob's surprise." Kathryn raised her head from her plate but directed her comments to the entire assembly. "Indeed, my lord," she answered in a quiet voice. "You can have little opinion of me if you think I should spoil his surprise in such a way." She finally turned her face to him, but her eyes remained hidden. "Since this afternoon, Jacob has spoken of nothing but the hope of a visit to the nursery where he may show you the surprise himself."

Dalton did not know why, but her answer pleased him immensely. An attention seeker would have taken full advantage of the opportunity he had thrust her way to dominate the conversation and bring complete notice upon her. But Miss Montgomery was made of sterner stuff, it seemed. She had no desire to spoil the delight of a child. Indeed, her answer pleased him beyond measure.

When the gentlemen decided they would forgo their brandy and cigars to join the ladies in the drawing room, he was looking forward to finding a chair as close to the engaging companion as he could. He did not make that observation lightly; after years on the Continent, he was an excellent judge of character, and he knew he had found a kindred spirit despite not being able to read her eyes.

He saw that Miss Charity seated herself on a love seat near the fire, and her look beckoned him to the spot beside her. He pretended not to notice.

He turned and saw Miss Montgomery standing in the farthest corner of the room. It would have put her quite beyond the pale had he joined her there. Dalton knew it was where she wished to be, and knowing he was being completely selfish, he said, "Miss Montgomery, perhaps you would like this chair a little closer to the fire. I see it remains quite empty."

He saw her turn to him in complete surprise. It was not in the corner of the room, but it was not in the center, either. He thought they could agreeably converse without appearing secluded. She approached the chair, appearing somewhat wary of him.

"I promise I shall not eat you, Miss Montgomery," he said, hoping to interject some levity.

"My lord, I did not mean to appear ungrateful!"

"You did not. There is something I particularly wished to ask you. I hope you will not think me forward."

Seating herself, she replied, "I cannot imagine what might interest you that one of the others might answer just as easily."

Was she in fear of retribution from her charge? He would not allow it. He would talk to whomever he pleased, and he would give the chit the set down she deserved if necessary.

"There are many things, I assure you." He stood a little apart from her chair, making sure there were no codes of conduct broken for a drawing room discourse. "I wondered about your eyes." She did not look at him, but pushed the spectacles against the bridge of her nose anxiously. "I do not mean to pry. I assumed it to be a condition involving light, but as you are wearing them this evening, I see that cannot be the reason. May I ask if it is something more serious?"

She stuttered for a moment; he had taken her quite

off guard. "I…I… No, it has nothing to do with the intensity of light, my lord. My spectacles are for quite another purpose, not one I should like to go into at present. You may suffice it to say that they are the bane of my existence!" She did smile at that, so her refusal did not come with any malice or indication she was not pleased with him.

Indeed, he continued quite comfortably. "Then may I change subjects and ask you if the Dinsmores attend church on Sundays? I was pleasantly surprised to find the rector joining us for dinner, though he was not apt to speak overmuch."

"The family does not attend church on any regular basis, I am afraid. But it is not far from here, and I can easily give you its direction."

He smiled. "Does the good parson have more to say from his pulpit than he had at dinner?" He did not wish to appear to be belittling the gentleman so added, "Perhaps he was in a thoughtful state of mind tonight?"

"No, no, my lord, he is quite reserved at all times." She kept her eyes forward, but he could see a small smile. She had not mistaken his first question. "If you wish for a good fire-and-brimstone sermon, I am afraid you are doomed to disappointment."

He laughed. "I would prefer something a little more in the middle, but I will let God handle what He feels I need to hear." Somehow the next question was one he knew he wanted the answer to, but he did not realize it until this moment. "Do you attend services, ma'am?"

She sighed. "I am sorry to disappoint you on this front, as well. I believe God has quite given up on me, my lord. I have not done so for many years." It was as if she knew he would ask more, so she turned the subject. "I presume you have attended St. George's in London? I never got the chance, rather, I did not get the opportunity to view the church from the inside."

"It is quite beautiful, to be sure. But there are times when I feel like the ones preaching there are a little prideful of their pulpit and make themselves of more consequence than their message."

He waited for some comment from her, but none came. It appeared she did not wish to discuss God, though she had alluded to a time when she did.

"I did not visit many places, but I believe Richmond Park was—"

Charity interrupted rudely. "My lord, shall I play the pianoforte for you? You may turn the pages for me, if you would be so kind."

He'd had more than enough of this spoiled child and her impoliteness, especially as it was more often than not aimed at her companion. He bristled and said, "Miss Charity, I am presently—"

This time it was Miss Montgomery who interrupted *him*. "Charity, I am sure that will make Lord Dalton feel quite like he is in a fashionable drawing room in London." She turned to him. "You must excuse me, my lord. I have a few things I promised to prepare for the children in the morning. I will say good-night."

She rose and bowed her head to him, then walked to the middle of the room and curtsied while she spoke small words of "excuse me" and "sleep well." She even asked Charity if there was anything else she could do for her that evening. Dalton watched her leave the room, certain now that she had not wished to upset her spoiled charge.

He found himself getting angry. All at once he realized that perhaps that was the lot of a companion. He had met many each Season, but he had thought no more about them once the introductions had been made. Miss Montgomery was a lady. She had a past of some sort among the *ton;* she had told him so herself. To be relegated to such a position must be most degrading.

Worse yet, the only reason he noticed her was because he appreciated her conversation and preferred her to any other person in this household. God pricked his heart. He should treat everyone equally no matter their position in life, yet he had excluded an entire middle class, neither servant nor member of the peerage. He would change that, beginning now.

His thoughts were interrupted *again* by the beauty clearing her throat.

"I would be delighted to turn the pages for you," he replied, with gritted teeth. Even this chit must be treated equally, he supposed. Only she surprised him and stopped playing. "Oh, my lord, this is too boring. I wish to give you some exciting news."

"Charity?" her mother said, dragging out her name in question.

"Mama, I have thought of the very thing! We must throw a ball while Lord Dalton is here!"

"A ball?" cried Lady Dinsmore and Lord Dalton at precisely the same time.

"Perhaps not a *ball* per se, but we could have a party

where we may introduce his lordship to our neighbors. And we may have music and dance the night away." She ended this by twirling around with eyes closed like a child.

"Lady Dinsmore, I protest. I would never put you to so much trouble on my behalf. I specifically told Sir John I would not wish any such attention."

"Sir John and I *did* speak of having a small dinner party while you were here, and should the children wish to roll back the rugs for a few dances, I should not object. We shall discuss it further when Sir John is free. And you cause us no trouble, whatsoever. Miss Montgomery has always been a big help to me in such areas. I quite look on her for all guidance when it comes to matters of Society."

He was forced to allow the subject to drop, but he decided he would quit this room as soon as possible. He had feigned tiredness from a full day of riding, so excused himself when the tea tray arrived.

So here he was, alone in his room at the unseemly hour of ten o'clock. His Bible lay open on his lap. *Lord, I only want to be free of this place. Perhaps You have brought me here for some purpose? Give me Your peace and grace to stay when impatience begs me to flee. And Lord, help me to focus on You and Your will as I face so many distractions.*

He was distracted indeed. He could not stop thinking about the woman on the bridge last night. She caused so many emotions in his breast.

She was amazing! Her voice was rich and calming. Her bearing was regal; she was a lady, of that he was certain. He knew it was odd of him, considering it was he who asked her to come, but he was concerned about her visiting the bridge alone so late at night. What if he had taken her second visit as an invitation to something more? She was defenseless.

He was very attracted to her, and he was happy that he could in no way attribute that to her physical appearance. He used to tell himself often that even had Lady Kathryn not been so beautiful, he would still have been drawn to her. But because she *was* so beautiful, he really never knew that for certain.

But this fairy could be hideous—which would explain the hood—and he would still be attracted to her. She made him laugh. That had become very important to him. Even the most beautiful woman's features would one day fade. He needed so much more in common with someone.

Only look at his preference for Miss Montgomery. When unencumbered by her charge, she was delightful. And even when the chit was near, he believed Miss Montgomery sensed his feelings easily and shared them, if only with a simple smile.

He had not chased after the woman last night. He did not want to snatch midnight meetings with her. He wanted to find her, get to know her. Sight unseen, she was too special to let go.

As Kathryn laid down her brush and donned her cotton night rail, she supposed she would just have to be herself—herself in a foolish wig, shoes and spectacles—and wait for the fortnight to end. She had no delusions, even after such short acquaintance; there would be no marriage between Lord Dalton and Charity. It was also clear he was already trying to invent ways to shorten his stay at the manor and decrease the amount of time he must politely spend with its inhabitants. Perhaps she would be lucky, and he would abort his stay and return to London. Yet a pang touched her heart at the thought.

Her life had changed so that his presence should be of absolutely no importance to her. And now, despite her sheer weariness of an hour ago, she was wide-awake, staring at the ceiling. She could not go downstairs for a book; she had only just left the drawing room complaining she could not keep her eyes open.

Suddenly she perked up, and the wheels in her mind began to turn. Could she go to the bridge? It was not yet ten o'clock; the family would be ensconced in the drawing room at least another hour with their guest. The locals never used the bridge after dark, no matter what the time. Indeed, witches, gnomes and trolls were her friends!

Even as she questioned herself, she rooted through her drab dresses to find her rumpled walking dress of the previous night. By the time she finished hooking the buttons on the serviceable gown, she was resolved to get some fresh air.

She cherished her nighttime freedom, though she had never gone two nights in a row, much less three. Once a week was all she dared risk. But her pistol had given her courage, and once she knew the freedom, even rarely, she could not give it up.

Kathryn was not a fool. She did not dismiss the fact that Lord Dalton might also take a late-night walk to the bridge. She would not put it past him to assume she was a local wench who would also be on the look-out for him. But she felt secure in the knowledge that she would be back long before he retired for the night. Even should he claim fatigue after the drawing room and not join Sir John privately for brandy and billiards, she had at least an hour.

The thought cheered her as none had that day. She would allow herself this one extra hour of complete freedom before she subjected herself to the next fort-night of frustration and the knowledge that had she not allowed Lord Salford to whisk her away, she might even belong to Lord Dalton today.

Kathryn slipped her dark cloak over her shoulders, pulled the hood loosely up over her head and left her room. She looked both ways and took the hallway to the servant's staircase to the kitchen, where she could slip out unnoticed.

His Bible was doing him little good this night. He could not concentrate on the words for all of the noise in his head.

He could not sit still any longer; he had to get out of this room. He would walk to the bridge again. He knew it was far too early to expect his late-night visi-tor, if indeed she intended to visit at all. That was not his purpose in going. He only wanted some air.

So he took up his position at last night's tree, listen-ing to the gurgling water and taking in deep breaths of the country breezes. He could not resume his search for his fairy, but if there was any chance of seeing her or finding out her identity, he would take it.

Dalton's thoughts were interrupted by the sound of a scream, cut off hastily, on the other side of the bridge. As he pushed away from the solid trunk and stepped quietly onto the ancient structure, the sight that met his eyes stopped his heart.

Chapter Five

Dalton froze. It was her, the woman he had met last night, but in no way situated as he had imagined. There on the other end of the span, less than one hundred feet from him, she stood with her head held tightly against the bridge's stone pillar with a hand covering her mouth. Dalton could only be thankful that the hood that covered her head might provide a small cushion as her attacker held her so tightly against the stones.

She was imprisoned by the weight of a man's body, and her neck arched to avoid the knife pressed dangerously close to her skin. He could tangibly feel her terror.

He pulled up short, his heart no longer stopped, but beating very fast. *Dear Lord, You are more than capable of protecting this woman, but if Your way of protecting her involves me, show me the way.* He had hoped to surprise her attacker by stealth, but the woman saw him from under the folds of her hood. That single glance in his direction gave his presence away.

The man wielding the knife had complete control

over the woman, but he turned his lecherous gaze to Lord Dalton. "Stay where ye are or I'll slit 'er throat, don't think I won't. Even in the dark, it looks too purty to scar."

The cur's voice was raspy and common, and Dalton heard the girl's slight whimpers as he pushed the point of his dagger just a little farther into her skin.

"Let her go," Dalton said, his command in deadly earnest. Anyone who knew him would have followed those orders instantly. His opponent, however, though now more hesitant, did not know enough to recognize the menace in his words.

Instead, the assailant laughed and seemed to wedge his knee tighter against the woman's fragile frame, effectively pinning her closer and, no doubt, making breathing even more difficult for her. "It don't seem to me you be the one in the position to be hagglin' now does it? Looks like this be my lucky night. I found me a purty wench with a rich cove to pay for 'er life!"

"There will be no bargaining. You will let her go or I will kill you." Evil was evil, whether in wartime or not.

Dalton thought the woman would be in shock. She kept rolling her head from side to side, trying to get away from the grimy hand that covered her mouth. The attacker only pushed a little harder on his knife to make her stop each time.

"Mighty uppity you are when it's me what 'as the knife." Her attacker laughed. "Now jest toss me your purse," the man continued, "then back off. Ye get on that 'orse of yours and ride away. Ye do all that and the 'arpy comes out of this with a whole skin."

His voice held no fear, and Dalton knew this was the worst kind of enemy.

He was screaming so close to the woman that she jumped, feeling the knife as she did so. "Do what I say, *now*—'er life makes no never mind to me." With that he actually punctured her skin with the tip of the blade and sniggered as blood trickled down her neck.

Her cry led him to comply. He removed his purse from his coat and tossed it to the center of the bridge. He could have thrown it as far as the man's feet, but he wanted the cutthroat to come and get it.

The release of his coins seemed to lighten her attacker's mood, if not his hold. "Sounds 'eavy enough. Might even be all I need for this night's work and I can give meself a little reward. Ol' Jack Dawkins might even let this wench live." He became deadly serious once more. "Now pick up the brass and toss it all the way to me...don't make me kill 'er."

Dalton knew if he could keep the man distracted, there was more of a chance that he would slip up, giving him an opportunity get the woman away safely. If that did not happen, Dalton was more than prepared to face the man's knife. But it must first be pointed at him instead of the fairy.

Suddenly the night burst into a flurry of sounds and movement that took all three participants by surprise.

She had been telling the truth! She *was* armed and, apparently, not afraid to use her weapon.

The flash of powder and the crack of the pistol sounded like thunder in the quiet night. But the scream of pain and the surprise of the counterattack allowed her to push against him with all her might. Dalton ran toward the man, ready to kill him if necessary, but he was stopped by the woman who ran straight into his arms.

He held her so tightly that his anger abated for a moment at the thought of her being safe and secure in his grasp, as if she belonged there.

But reality flooded back when Ol' Jack began howling. "She shot me! The 'ussy shot me!" Her attacker lifted the arm he had been using to cover her mouth, and examined his wound. It was clear that the bullet had entered the man's lower left side, and he was growling in pain.

Dalton could see the hole in the back of the man's coat, however, and knew their troubles were not yet over; the bullet must have grazed his side before exiting the back of the man's grimy jacket. There was no debilitating damage.

As pain and anger filled the eyes of the ruffian, Dalton knew they might as well be dealing with a wounded bear, and he determined nothing would prevent him from protecting the frightened woman in his arms. His military training took over, and he was a force to be reckoned with. He gripped her upper shoulders tightly, moving her quickly behind him.

"Your light-skirt ain't done nothin' but caused 'er own death and I don't care if I 'ave to go through ten of you to get to 'er." His voice was a slow growl, the sound of an injured animal. He tossed his knife back and forth between his hands then began to charge Dalton, thrusting his dagger, wildly intent on murder.

But Dalton was more than prepared, and with one

swift kick to the wrist of the injured thatchgallow, the knife went flying far into the high river grasses on the other side of the bridge.

Ol' Jack was stunned but not cowed. "No gentry cove is gettin' the best o' me," he swore, but was stopped short by the punishing left Dalton landed in the center of his face. The blood gushing into his mouth finally seemed to turn the tide. While Dalton prepared for whatever response the cutthroat threw at him next, Jack Dawkins turned on his heels and dashed away, doing the one thing Dalton did *not* expect. And Dalton had not been granted near enough time with the villain to assuage his anger.

As he prepared to follow the man, he took a quick look over his shoulder and stopped dead in his tracks. The brave young woman so recently in his arms had quietly slid to the ground into a sitting position, her back against the stone wall of the bridge. Her head was down on her pulled-up knees, and she was shrouded in her cloak. He could see, even from where he stood, that she shivered uncontrollably in silence. He had witnessed many shattering experiences in battle, but his heart had never been touched so deeply by any sight.

He lost all thought of pursuit, which angered him but did not eat at him as it once would have. Dawkins would more than likely not expire from his injuries, but he could never stop for a doctor. Not, at least, until he was very far from Trotton, and by then Dalton knew he would suffer a great deal, almost enough to make up for the lifetime of suffering he had caused Dalton and this woman in a matter of moments.

He very quietly went to her side and lowered himself onto one knee beside her. Dalton wanted so badly for her to know he was there to protect her as long as she wanted him. But he knew in his heart that she probably had little awareness of him as she dealt with her own inner struggles. He gently put one arm under her knees and the other around her back as he slowly, tenderly lifted her from the ground. She did not raise her head, and he tried not to be overly encouraged when she wrapped her arms tightly around his neck, as if holding on to him for dear life.

He walked off the bridge and over to a tree with a divided trunk, allowing him to settle them both between the huge limbs, almost as if wrapping themselves in another pair of arms: God's arms. The swaying branches effectively blocked them from any view and he leaned back, allowing her legs to settle on his lap as his arms tightened around her, holding her close to his chest, willing life back into her.

Her hands were fisted against his breast as if in perpetual preparation for a fight, and her head rested uneasily against his broad chest. He began to stroke her back, realizing as he did so that her hood had slipped down, and he rested his chin against the top of her head.

He whispered over and over, in the quietest of voices, "It is all right now. Nothing will hurt you. I have you safe." His mind raced for any comforting words that he might murmur to her, at the same time feeling so inadequate in his attempts to soothe her. *Lord, help me! Give me Your words, Your own comforting touch, whatever You feel she needs now; instill it in me for her benefit.*

Unable to bear her reticence any longer, and worried about the injury to her neck, he spoke to her in a voice filled with awe, against the top of her head. "You are the bravest woman I have ever seen. You were magnificent, my fairy, you were smart and wonderful in a terrible moment."

Dalton was wholly unprepared for the response his words wrought. It was as if actually speaking out loud broke her out of some protective shell she had placed around herself, and the floodgates opened. Her fists unclenched only long enough to grasp his lapels in a lifeline grip, and she turned her face into his chest and sobbed, a heart-wrenching pain…all in complete silence. He had never been so scared in all his life, fighting Bonaparte included.

He could feel the unrelenting rise and fall of her chest as she pulled in and released great breaths of air. But it was her tears, the silent sobs already dampening his shirtfront, that grabbed his heart with an emotion he had never felt before.

He only held her tighter, rocking gently as his cheek rested against her hair. Could he give her what she needed to get through this? He had never tried before. Many times he had had the unpleasant duty of informing a family at the loss of one of their men, but he had thought himself to be detached. He was detached. Yet this young woman made him wish he had learned to comfort in a way that would heal her physical as well as her emotional pain.

Slowly, and in the slightest of degrees, her sobbing eased and he realized that maybe time and a feeling of safety were all that he could give her. Maybe she had to let those inner demons painfully emerge, or she would have stayed in that shell as she had been on the bridge—shut out of the world and quickly building a wall to keep it out. This lovely woman had the presence of mind to release herself from a most dangerous situation before he had been able to do so. Now she was dealing with the emotional aspect of that action in a way more touching than he could have imagined.

Her sobs finally stopped, and he thankfully felt the small stages of release as she relaxed her tightly wound body ever more as the moments passed. Her breathing finally evened for such a long time that had her grip not remained strong and tight on his lapels, he might have believed her to have fallen into an exhausted slumber.

At this moment, however, he knew only aggravation, a futility that he could not carry her home in safety without breaking the peaceful and calming silence she had instigated.

"I must get you home. You need to be warmed by a fire, and your poor neck must be attended to." He felt her begin to tense, so he began his gentle ministrations again, rubbing her back and whispering softly. "We will go very slowly. I will not jar you more than necessary. But you must tell me where to go. You may then relax and think no more of it. I will take care of everything."

"No," said the voice, so low he was not even sure she had spoken it.

"I hope you know I would give all I own to be able to hold you safe like this, but you will catch your death and we must bandage your wound. I will not leave you."

"No," she said again, shaking her head.

Dalton sighed but could not resist her. For the second time in his life, he evidenced the power a woman could wield over a man. It was unsettling. He vowed no woman would break his heart as Kathryn had.

She sat up and pulled back to look into his face. He thought she might regret being there with him, but he somehow believed she knew she would never need to be afraid of him.

"Sir, I owe you my life," she began softly.

"No, I did nothing, you…" he began, but she stopped him with a hand to his lips.

Her touch brought on the desired silence.

She sniffled once again as he heard tears in her voice. He thought she was cried out. "I have nothing with which to repay you for my life, and even less with which to thank you for your…for this time. I promise you," she continued, "I have never received such careful attention from another, and I will never forget it, never."

He lowered his eyes to her neck and tried to make out the seriousness of the wound. He thought it would heal with little care, but he knew it to be painful, nonetheless. He gently reached a finger up to touch it and felt the rhythmic pulse that beat so quickly as his finger rested there. She was not as brave as she let on; her fear was still present.

She shook her head and brushed back his hand. "It is but a scratch compared to what could have happened. I will look upon it in the future and remember the blessing you have given to me instead of the horror of this night."

She slid out of his arms and faced him, but he kept hold of her to steady her.

"You are correct, sir. I must go. But please, please accept my…heart…" she said intently, then looked away and cleared her throat, "my heartfelt thanks. I will never forget all you have done for me tonight."

A sudden gust of wind blew the branches of the tree, allowing the moonlight to shine on them, illuminating their hiding place. He finally got a glimpse of her face, and he wanted to memorize her features.

What? He stared into the eyes she did not realize were uncovered. His hold of both her arms increased in intensity. "Kathryn?" He thought it must be a trick of the moon. He felt her tense in his arms.

"It *is* you!" He pulled her fully into his arms, holding her so tightly, unable to stop. Nine years slipped away as nothing, only now he knew he must hold her and never let her go.

He felt her grab on to his labels and turn her face into his chest. It was her. Kathryn. He could not see her clearly, but the moonlight had shown him enough. And she smelled so good. Would he ever forget that scent?

Wait. He *had* smelled it again, *recently. Think, think,* he ordered himself. It was…it was Miss Montgomery! What was going on here?

Suddenly he moved her back to his arm's length and stared into her eyes. She tried to pull free, and when she could not, she turned her face away.

"Oh, no you don't." He grabbed her chin with one

hand and held it steady, staring into the eyes of the one woman he had thought never to see again.

"Well, well, Lady Kathryn," he said with clenched teeth. "What game are you playing this time?"

Chapter Six

Kathryn's first feelings when he pulled her to him were of hope. She felt as if she were home, where she belonged. But those feelings changed to fear and embarrassment at his words. How could she have let this happen? Two weeks, that was all—if she had just remained in her room for a fortnight, he would never have known. God still held a grudge, it seemed, and she had been stupid to test it.

At least she was to finally learn what would happen if he knew.

"I want an explanation. And I want the truth, if you please." His arms still held her like a vise, and he used his power to make her stand perfectly still. But he could not wait for an explanation from her, it seemed. He was trying to make sense of it on his own.

"You… This cannot be." She watched him, wary of what he would say next. "You and the companion… you smell the same. Are you masquerading here?" He shook his head, trying to understand, she supposed. She doubted he ever could.

"You wore this scent…back then. I could not place it on this woman, on you, until now. And the companion, Miss Montgomery, she wears it, as well. What game is this?" He said the last through clenched teeth, not realizing the grip on her arms would leave bruises tomorrow.

How could he remember her fragrance from nine years ago? If he only knew she was the woman on the bridge, she could have disappeared into Miss Montgomery, and he would never have found her again. But he remembered. Perhaps once past his initial anger, he would be happy to see her.

"What in the blazes is going on, Lady Kathryn?" He spoke her name as if it made him sick to say it. "Tell me the truth."

"You already know most of the truth. I have never outright lied to you. I realize the sin of omission is not much different, but I did what I had to do."

"Your definition of truth seems to be quite at odds with mine, *Miss Montgomery*."

She tried to stem the anger that rose in her as he became dreadful. She balled her hands into fists and said, with as much grace as she could muster, "You have made your point, my lord. You know my name is Kathryn. Please use it or not, but stop your reminder of my crime." This was so much harder than she had imagined. She had longed for the day when he would come to find her and would hold her hands and gently soothe her as she told him the truth. If that's what he wanted, then that is what he would get. All of it.

"You wish to berate me." She was no longer angry. She thought she had just faced the worst night of her life. All she wanted was to be safe and alone in her room. She even wanted to go back into the protective shell she wrapped around her on the bridge. But she knew now that the worst of this night was not over. "So be it. I deserve whatever you think of me."

"What you deserve is little to the point…madame."

Kathryn's heart sank further still, but she would not let him see it. She saw no sympathy, only an angry bitterness that would not rest. Very well, she had known from that first night on the Rother River Bridge that the truth would give him a disgust of her, so it mattered little now.

"What do you wish to know, sir?" she asked him quite coolly.

"Great guns, what do you think I wish to know?" The words were ground out between clenched teeth. He soon began pacing from the tree to her and back again. "Why the disguise? Why the Dinsmores? Why deceive me?"

The last was ground out directly into her face, and the force of his emotions made her step back.

She could see now how she had hurt him. She always prayed that it would not be so, but God seemed to take her prayers and turn them around until they were the complete opposite of what she asked for.

"I will explain anything you wish, if you will only

calm yourself." She was once again the practical Miss Montgomery trying to defuse a volatile situation.

"Get on with it, then," he growled.

"When my… When I determined I must make my own way in the world, I offered myself up into the two sacrificial positions allowed a lady—a companion and a governess." She would not start at the beginning.

"I tried to find employment in Sussex County, but I was always turned away. No household, they informed me, would hire me because I was too young and too…"

"Beautiful," he uttered, sitting down on the divided tree.

"You may use that word, my lord. I do not. My appearance has been a bane to my existence. I abhor the Society that expects all young women to be decorations for a man's arm and income to his pockets, yet takes advantage of those same qualities in women of a different class."

"You speak in riddles. What do you know of such things? Keep to the subject at hand."

Anger began to grow in her. "Of course, my lord. Forgive me for making you feel uncomfortable. A thousand pardons, I assure you. One of *my* class must remember her station!"

"What in the blazes are you talking about?" Her words were bringing on the wrong reactions, but she was angry, too. "Now is not the time to discuss the evils of our society. We were speaking of *your* specific actions."

"*Your* Society *is* the point, my lord. I could not look for a position in London because…well, you know why.

I was shunned. And I could not get employment in Sussex because the men of your class have no compunctions or morals with the women of mine. And because their wives, who do the hiring, know it!

"I was fired from several positions, after being turned down for as many, because of my appearance. My qualifications did not matter. My honesty, my integrity, my determination—none of it mattered. Even my need did not matter. The only thing that mattered was that I was young and passable and my person might provide temptation to the males of the household. Not that I might do so, but the way I looked. How do you fight that, my lord? *You* tell *me!*"

She sensed she was finally getting to him through her outpouring of anger and resentment. "It seems it is common knowledge that young wives did not want young, beautiful servants in their homes, but I did not know it." She poured out all of her pain on him.

His sarcasm abated somewhat. "Please continue, Lady Kathryn."

"I *had* to have employment, my lord." She was quieter now, giving details by rote with little emotion. "I had no choice." She leaned against the willow tree branch and crossed her arms over her chest as she looked past him to the moon. Should she tell him now why she had run away from London, from him, so long ago? "And having no choice due to my mistake, *my big mistake,* I determined that if appearance was hindering my options, I would change my appearance.

"Miss Mattingly and I concocted the awkward, ageless Miss Montgomery, and it worked. I held two very respectable positions with exactly the same credentials as I had always possessed, but my homeliness made all the difference. So you may scoff and sneer as you like, but I will not apologize for having to outwit Society to survive."

"I will grant you your disguise, then, Lady Kathryn, and allow you your reasons." The tic in his jaw became more noticeable as he growled the rest of this speech. "What I fail to see is why you felt it necessary to continue to lie to me once I had seen the real you on the bridge?"

"You will *grant* me...you will *allow* me? I am indebted to you, I assure you." Her sarcasm took her from quiet explanation to an angry lioness. But her tempest burned out quickly. "My lord, you know very well why I could not reveal myself to you. And how could I know that after meeting me on one occasion that you would again seek me out? You had no intimate knowledge of me, certainly nothing to warrant such persistence. And quite contrary to what you think, I planned as well as I could to avoid appearing as myself during your stay. I was not successful."

"One occasion? We met nine years ago! It could be the only answer as to why I was attracted to you."

"And that is why I could not tell you."

Oh, she did not wish to cry, she did not wish to cry! She tried to stay angry by telling him her hardships, but none of those had anything to do with him. It seemed her mistake would haunt her for the rest of her life, and trying to explain it to him was impossible when the only thing she wanted him to know was how sorry she was that she had left him.

He was so surprised to find her, much less masquerading as someone else, that he barely took in one of every three words she said. It seemed she was mad at the world, even more so at him, and he could not understand it. His analytical mind failed him. Shouldn't he be the one who was angry?

"You continue to speak in riddles! You seem to think I understand your barbs and your mysteries, but I assure you I do not."

He realized a sparring match with her, as enticing as that might be, would get him nowhere. He did not know how to respond to her when he did not comprehend her anger. What did she mean, she was *shunned*? There was obviously much she was not telling him, but he would die before he would ask her. He only looked at her with a raised brow and outstretched hands, waiting. Let her make of it what she would.

"Then we will stick to the subject of Dinsmore Manor. How could you determine you were attracted to me from knowing me so long ago with a cloak covering my face and in less than an hour's time?"

"Are you forgetting the occasions we met while you were Miss Montgomery? You knew who I was then— why not tell me the truth? I would not have given away your disguise once I understood why you were disguised in the first place! At any time you could have trusted me enough to tell me the truth. It would have been the honorable thing to do."

"You are right, it would have been the honorable thing to do. It is only fair that you should be allowed to denigrate me for my actions nine years ago. Unfortunately, I let my heart rule my head when I decided to take this walk tonight." She pulled her cloak close around her. The moon was very high in the sky. "And I will pay dearly for it."

Dalton turned impaling eyes on her. Her heart? Was she going to reveal that she still had feelings for him? Could he possibly believe her?

Though she continued to speak of things he did not wholly understand, such as her *mistake,* he had to fight the pride he felt in her at overcoming the obstacles she had faced at every turn. However, he must remind himself how she had duped him purposely, for no apparent reason.

His resentment returned as he realized she never even considered the hurt she might be causing him. She made it all sound so innocent, but it had changed his life forever.

He could not believe he was standing here with the woman whose memory had tortured him for so many years, only to come to this. She was ripping his heart out again. This night had gotten progressively worse.

"You gave no thought to the Dinsmores and what they might fear with a complete stranger in their midst."

His voice broke, and he coughed to cover the sound. "And you gave absolutely no thought to me when you pretended to be both women. You might have taken into consideration how your actions would disrupt my life."

"No!" she exclaimed, her hands balled into fists.

"I took you into consideration in every one of my actions. I did not want you to have to make decisions that an honest man could not. I did not want you to have to help me continue the lie to the Dinsmores. And I did not want to give you the opportunity to…reject me if I told you the truth."

She started to cry, and he wished he could understand which part had hurt her so badly. "You did not have to pretend as the cloaked woman, and you did not have to pretend as Miss Montgomery—or Lady Kathryn, for that matter! *You* were *you!*"

"You were Lady Kathryn all along. It was Miss Montgomery who was a phony. I was on the verge of a real friendship to a real person, and there was no need to keep up the pretense after that. You could have told me the truth!"

"How dare you?" Kathryn cried. "It is very easy for you to stand there and say you would have taken an explanation of my ruse without a second thought. I say you would have been as angry then as you are now. Since you were planning to leave by the end of the fortnight, I would have been left behind as the companion, not the lady." She wiped the tears on her cheeks and said softly, "Left behind again."

"Again? If you have had some heartache in the past I am sorry. But now we will never know what I would have done, will we? Because you gave me so little credit, does not make it so. However, as that was in some measure what I wished for, that we might get to know one another better, I can truthfully say I am well out of it. Miss Montgomery was much more to my taste."

"Now that you have your answers, you need never see nor think of me again."

She pushed away from the tree and came to stand directly before him, anger emanating from every fiber of her being. "You believed that I was *two* different women, and it seems only one of them is acceptable to you. I find it quite a shame that you are only *one* person, and the one is in *no* way acceptable to me."

She turned and walked away. "Good night, my lord," she called over her shoulder.

"And good riddance," he heard clearly, though it was said through tears.

She stopped and added, "I suppose my fate is in your hands. I will wake up in the morning to face it."

"Oh, no you don't!" He grasped Kathryn's arm from behind. "Walking away and running away has been your trademark, no more. I want the truth, and I intend to get it."

"You just said you had gotten what you came for," she ground out, and wrenched her arm from his hand.

"All I learned is that you were forced into employment, and that you had to dupe people into getting a position." He ran his hands through his hair out of frustration. "You have said much here tonight that I do not understand. I believe I need to hear the entire truth, what you are not telling me." He then looked into her eyes and softened his tone. He wished he did not need to know more. He had gone into the army solely for the purpose of putting it all behind him, but the need remained.

"Why did you leave me nine years ago?"

What had he said? Did he really not know what happened to her? "I do not understand you, my lord?"

"I believe it is a simple enough question."

"Are you asking me to believe that you do not know what happened after... When I left?" Kathryn's mind began to race. Could there have been some way in which the entire affair was hushed up? No, it would have been impossible. How would her father have explained away an elopement or her disappearance?

"I do not ask you to *believe* anything. You have said many things I do not understand. I can only assume you wish to keep them to yourself. But I feel you owe me or, rather, that I deserve to know why you disappeared." He seemed to *need* those answers. "I would like to know the entire truth so I may put my mind at rest. And I believe the best way will be from the beginning. However, it all depends on you. I cannot make you say what you will not."

"Oh, dear," she muttered under her breath. She could choose not to tell him and he would leave angry, but he would not leave hating her. He need only think badly of her action at the Dinsmores.

No. No more lies, no more hiding. It's time.

"My lord, perhaps it will help me if you can tell me the last thing you know about that Season." She so much wanted to hear about his entire experience during that time. Would he tell her whether or not he had developed feelings for her? She must not ask that of him; she only needed a place to start. Even that would no longer be important; he would not like what he was about to hear no matter where she started. But as he began to speak, she waited.

"Very well. We were a full two months into your first Season. We spent quite a lot of time together, and I thought you enjoyed my company as I did yours. I hoped… I thought… Confound it—it does not matter what I thought. One day I called at your home, and the house appeared to be completely shut up. I could find no reason for this over the next few days. Some said your family had received bad news and had gone back to the country. Others said they had heard you and your father went abroad. Most had no news of you at all."

Kathryn could not comprehend this. How had her father arranged it all so deftly? He was certainly an intelligent and capable man, but to move the entire household back to Montgomery Hall in one day? And what of Lord Salford? He knew the truth and could have made her look even blacker.

"I wrote to your father at Montgomery Hall expressing my concern for you and your family, but I received no reply." His voice rose, she thought, in anger. "So I joined the regiment at the end of the Season. I was there four years, and when my brother died, I sold out and spent the next few years learning to run the estate and taking care of my mother."

He could have left it at that. Did he care for her more than he had shown her? She doubted it. So why did he need to know about this now?

"Do you mind if I sit down?" she asked him. He had risen from the branch, and frankly, she was tired.

He seemed to forget about the attack in all of this. "Do you remember Lord Salford?" she asked baldly.

"The name does not ring a bell. Should it?"

So antagonism would be his attitude. Very well, she would explain it and they would be done. "I met him at a ball about a month after we arrived in Town. He asked me to marry him."

She thought she heard an intake of breath, but she decided she would get this out, then try to return her life to some sort of normalcy. "He told me he would die if he could not have me." She laughed as she thought about that now. If anyone knew you did not die of a broken heart, she did. "I was young and stupid, and he convinced me we should elope."

This time, it was not just an intake of breath. He walked to stand in front of her on the branch. "You agreed to an elopement?" The shock in his voice could not be disguised. When she looked up at him, the moon was behind him and she could not see his face. With his size and voice, she could easily have believed him to be an angel from God, reminding her of her unforgivable mistake.

"Yes, my lord, I eloped. I flatter myself that I thought I was truly loved. However, that is still no reason to elope." She turned away from what she imagined would be in his eyes if she *could* see them. "If you will recall, I was not yet eighteen. He told me it was our only option if we wished to be together."

He turned his back on her. She closed her eyes, trying to keep tears at bay. There had been enough tears to last a lifetime. Though she had always known he would turn his back on her, she had never imagined it quite so literally. She would not stop; she would reveal it all. "We spent days speeding toward Gretna Green. He was afraid my father was following us." She had to laugh at that, too. Her father wanted nothing to do with her.

"It appears he knew my father better than I did. An outrider met us outside of the little inn that was to be our honeymoon idyll. He had one letter for Lord Salford and one letter for me." She stopped, wondering if he was even listening any longer. "My lord, I am sure you are not interested in the gory details. That is what you needed to know, is it not?"

"Go on," he said abruptly, his back still to her.

"My letter was quite brief. My father informed me that I was no longer his daughter and that my things would arrive over the following few days." She thought Lord Dalton did not stand so tall or have his head so high for a moment, but her tears welled up in the remembering of it, so she did not spare many thoughts on him. "I was more afraid than I have ever been in my life, but I thought God would protect me through my new husband.

"Lord Salford's missive, however, was much more informative. It seems he was counting on the receipt of my inheritance upon reaching my majority. My father was happy to inform him that I did not receive my inheritance until I was five and twenty. He was outraged and sure that my father would change his mind once we were married." Her tears flowed freely now, but as he could not see them, she did not care.

"He was not, however, as sure as he led me to believe. It seemed the truth had begun to sink in, and when he told me to wait in the parlor while he bespoke our rooms, he stole one of Father's carriage horses and rode off into the night. I never saw him again.

"As I have already explained, I spent the next few years taking positions, being groped, manhandled, lied about and fired from each one. When Matty came up with the disguise, she believed God was providing a way that would allow me to gain employment that would last as long as my charges grew up, in the case of a governess, or died, in the case of a companion. From God? I never thought so. He could not forgive the mistake I made."

She was ready for this to be over. "I was bound to be found out at some point in my life. I suppose God chose this one for some purpose, but as He is rather put out with me, I have no doubt it was to shame me further."

"And your father? Where is he?"

"I do not know. I *do* know, however, that he has always been implacable. I never doubted his love for me as we spent all those years without my mother. But that same love demanded something in return. I discovered it was conditional love, and I had no desire to be rejected by him a second time."

There was complete silence for what seemed an eternity. He finally broke it. "So you left me for another man and did not have the decency to let me know you did not return my feelings."

His feelings? Was he saying he *had* loved her?

"You not only left me, you eloped—something an honorable woman would never have agreed to." She flinched, but she did not respond; she deserved it.

"And you spent days *and nights* alone with him without the bonds of matrimony. You chose complete ruination over me."

Her pain increased one hundred fold. She had lived a complete lie for the past nine years. She had been manhandled and rejected in position after position. She had lost her father and the man she had loved. And he focused on one thing: *her big mistake.* Her ruination.

"Lady Kathryn," he said through clenched teeth, "I will bid you goodbye."

She watched him walk away from her through the tears in her eyes, and she knew he was gone for good. She had lost her reputation, her father and him. How would she survive this?

Chapter Seven

Two weeks later, Dalton sat alone in his library after an evening of cards with his friends. He was not foxed, but he drank enough tonight that he had no control over his heart, and his feelings came to the surface like a bubbling caldron.

He was tired. And though he had tried to overcome it in London, he was still angry at her. Indeed, it seemed to increase with time. How could he have been so dimwitted? He had worked with Wellington himself, yet could not see Lady Kathryn through a wig and spectacles! He put his head in his hands. He captured spies with such elaborate costumes they were almost impenetrable. She had fooled him with a wig, glasses and a voluminous cape.

Every angle of her features had been etched into his heart years ago. And because it was so, none other had been able to penetrate his heart.

He could tell himself it was because so much time had passed and she was the last person he expected to see, but he prided himself on his military training. He thought it was always with him; apparently he was wrong, and that made him a failure. She had made a laughingstock out of him, even if it was only in his mind. *Lord, how does one go about forgiving that?*

Her story had been so fantastic that it was hard to believe. But she could not have made up the things she spoke of. She would not have known about those things had she not experienced them. And contrary to what he had said, it broke his heart.

He did not want it to. He did not want to care what happened to her at all. But she had left him to *elope.* How had her father kept that secret for so long? He had spent weeks trying to discover her whereabouts.

This fortnight in London had been hard. He did not wish to give rise to talk, so he could not tell anyone. He wanted to be sure to protect her reputation, even as his heart balked at it.

He knew she had been waiting for some indication of what he felt for her then. He would not give her the satisfaction. As far as he was concerned, she would never know that he had fallen in love with her after only two months' acquaintance.

He remembered the exact moment he had recognized it as love. They were waltzing, always his happiest times with her.

"Have I told you how very beautiful you are tonight, Lady Kathryn?"

"Yes, my lord, you have." She looked up into his eyes and laughed. *"Only about one hundred times. I was beginning to think you did not notice."*

They had always enjoyed easy laughter. He loved that it came so natural to her.

"How can I make it up to you?"

"Say you will take me riding in the morning. I hate going during the afternoon crush when all that matters is what you are wearing and who you are with. I wish to gallop. And Gypsy told me only this morning that she will seek new ownership if she does not get one soon."

"I certainly cannot disappoint Gypsy, now can I?"

She looked up at him with adoration, or so he thought, and he fell under the spell of her sapphire-blue eyes, where he knew he would remain forever.

"Lady Kathryn, you continue to stare at my chest rather than my chiseled face."

She smiled up at him.

"While looking there, did you happen to notice my new stickpin?"

"Actually, my lord, I was admiring the intricate details of your cravat."

"Minx! If you will look a little closer, you will see a sapphire stickpin holding the mesmerizing folds."

"It is beautiful. I like it very much."

He spoke next in a low, soft whisper. "It reminded me of the most beautiful blue eyes I have ever seen. I think of them each time I look in the mirror to add the finishing touch."

Those eyes spoke volumes to him. They convinced him that she felt the same. But he could not talk of his feelings in the middle of a dance floor.

"Someday, I will introduce her to you."

Her initial shock gave way to a devious smile. "Be

careful, my lord, that you do not end up hoisted by your own petard."

His laughter turned the heads of dancers close by.

"Kathryn, you are making a public spectacle of us."

"You called me Kathryn."

"Did I? I am sorry. I thought that was your name."

"I have been wishing to ask you for weeks now if you would call me by my Christian name."

"I suppose I needed to know it was...the right time."

That made her blush. He kept trying to remember how young she was, but she had been the woman of her father's household since her mother died. She had only been twelve, so she seemed so much older than her years.

"Do you think you could call me Christopher, my sweet Kathryn?"

"No, my lord, that would not be proper, especially in my first Season. But I will think of you as such." She smiled, and he could see into her soul through her eyes. He was sure she was awakening to feelings she had not known before, but he did not want to scare her.

"Dalton, then, I insist. No more 'my lording' me."

"Very well, Dalton."

And his heart became permanently hers.

Looking back on it now, he did not know what to think. She was still the most beautiful woman he had ever seen, but her maturity had enhanced it somehow. He could not deny that, as much as he wished to.

But he could deny he had any feelings for her now. To be so deceptive went against everything he believed in. She had eloped! He wanted to say he was well out of it; that it was such a reprehensible course of action, but somehow that she chose to leave him was worse and it injured his heart. That had been her choice—a choice she made freely.

He could understand why she felt that donning a disguise had been necessary. She had been through some of the lowest part of a Society that believes it acceptable to prey on women in the lower orders. In his hazy condition he wanted to make that right for her. He wanted what he always wanted—to love and protect her from any hardship.

No! He could not change what happened to her, and she had not told him the truth. For three days she had had an opportunity to do so and had not. He would not say "poor, pitiful me" as he swiped away an angry tear. He would put the blame where it belonged, on her.

Yet tonight, memories of the past would not let go of him.

They had taken a drive to Richmond Park one glorious day, and they had shared themselves completely.

"Kathryn, I have had thoughts of nothing but the army since I was a lad. I am beginning to believe that you have changed all of that."

"No, my lord, I would not wish to be the cause of a broken dream, no one would. You would one day wonder how your life would have been different had you gone to fight for your country. You must tell me more about it. I know so little about the war."

"I did not bring it up to sully your ears, my sweet."

"Please do not treat me like a child. In what way do you want to serve?"

"I have dreamed of a cavalry regiment."

"You wish to be in the thick of things, then?"

He was surprised at her understanding. He kept thinking of her as too young.

"I suppose so, but not for glory or the way the uniform looks. I want to fight for England from the tyranny of Bonaparte. I want to clear a path for the foot soldiers to get through." He had not wanted a discussion about the war. He wanted to let her know he thought only of her now. "I do not wish to ruin the joy of our ride."

"I will worry about you in such danger. But I will be so very proud to know you."

But his dream waned when he realized he wanted to marry her. He wanted to be near her, take care of her. With his education, he thought he could get a position in the War Office in London. He had planned it all.

But she cared for his dreams so little that she agreed to an elopement…an elopement with Lord Salford!

He had not remembered him during their conversation two weeks ago; he had been in shock by his surprise at finding her there. But he remembered Salford now. Everyone knew he was a lecherous fortune hunter. Everyone, it seemed, but Lady Kathryn. He was twenty years older than she, at a minimum!

His anger changed to more maudlin thoughts. How could she have chosen Salford over him? He had fallen in love with her. She was so young; he wanted her to understand real love. He wanted to teach her that. Apparently, she had found a more practiced suitor.

He now knew why pride was such an easy sin to commit, and why it was an easy sin to sustain. It had happened nine years ago when she left him. And it happened again when she told him of Lord Salford. And he had reacted the same way both times: he had run away. He thought of the irony—they seemed to have that in common.

So he had run again, this time to Rye to visit his mother and meet with his steward, to leave London and the memories of their time there together behind him.

After settling Merlin into his stall, he entered the house, purposing to go straight to his room until he could calmly be with his mother. He still needed time to think. Kathryn was not the woman he thought he knew, and there was the rub—apparently she never had been.

As he passed the drawing room, his mother was leaving it and she smiled, delighted to see him. "Christopher, I did not expect to see you so soon. I thought that you would be in London longer after you left Sir John's."

"I did go to London for a time. There was a matter I needed to take care of. It is done, and I will return to Town in a few days."

"Is something wrong, love?"

"It is something I must work through. I will overcome it— I must. Do not worry."

"Let us go where we may talk. If you have something to sort out, it always helps to have another perspective, someone to listen while you talk it out."

"I think not, Mother. It is done."

"I shall not press you, then. I will see you at breakfast?"

"Of course."

The next morning was still too soon to be in his mother's company, but too late to leave her now. He would excuse himself to take care of estate business and be more prepared to face her the next time.

But that is not how it transpired.

"Christopher, I would like you to sit with me awhile."

He did not ask for a second reprieve. In truth, he was so troubled he thought he needed another's counsel. *Her* counsel.

She sat in her damask-covered chair near the fire. He went to the mantel and stared down into it. She left it to him to begin the conversation, but he knew she would not be still long.

"Mother, I do not even know where to start."

"Maybe you should start at the beginning."

"I met a woman in Trotton. I was intrigued, but it was Kathryn."

"My goodness, Kathryn haunts you still?"

He laughed at how closely she came to the truth while never being further from it.

"No ma'am, it actually *was* Lady Kathryn." He sat down in the chair next to hers, eyes still lost in the fire. She did not cry out in surprise. She did not even urge him to continue. He loved her for that.

"Once I start, I fear I will not be able to stop. You will find it preposterous. I give you fair warning."

"I have nowhere to go, my dear. I *wish* to hear it all."

He spent the next two hours sitting, pacing and explaining all that had happened at Dinsmore Manor. He told her about Kathryn's masquerade, not only as the lady on the bridge but as the companion to Miss Charity. "It was all her. Miss Montgomery and the woman on the bridge were the same woman—Lady Kathryn."

Even his mother could no longer keep her countenance. "Oh, my darling, what a shock for you! Did she explain why? I do not see why she would lie to *you*." He knew she would understand his pain, she always had.

He tried to stop the catch in his voice, but each time he thought of it, as many new emotions tugged at his heart. He walked to the window that looked out on pristine lawns.

He felt her hand on his shoulder, and she said, "Then you do not know why she felt the need for the charade? I can only guess at your imaginings."

"No, Mother, there is more." He led her back to the sofa and joined her there. "I was determined to hear the truth."

"Then you *do* know why she went to such lengths to keep her identity a secret." It was a statement, not a question. "You know why she left London so many years ago."

"Yes, I do." He sat forward and leaned his elbows on his knees. His legs began a nervous bounce. "She eloped." He waited for his mother's reaction, but none was forthcoming. He went on in a harsher voice. "She eloped with the lecherous Lord Salford. She left me for him." Again he expected a gasp, an intake of breath, something to show she shared his vehemence. Very well; he would make a clean breast of it. "When her father discovered their intent, he disowned her. The fortune-hunting Salford left her unwed and ruined at Gretna Green."

This time the reaction came, but it was not what he expected. "Oh, that poor girl!"

He stood, staring down at her in disbelief. "That poor girl? That poor girl? Is that all you have to say?"

"Christopher, calm down. I am not your enemy. I assume there is much more to the story than that."

He apologized to her but was still frustrated. He wanted her to be as angry at Kathryn as he was. He told her the reason she went into hiding, disguising herself with the wig and spectacles. She closed her eyes as he told her of the unwanted attentions she had been forced to accept in her new status. And he told her that she had been in a closed carriage for days and nights on the road with Salford. Alone. She was ruined. There, that would do it.

"I can see how very angry you are over this. I suggest you let me think on it. We should both spend some time in prayer, and perhaps we may discuss this rationally."

"Rationally? Mother, there is nothing rational about this entire affair. You are more affected by her plight than mine, and I cannot credit it." He finally heard himself. He was acting like a spoiled child when things did not go his way. Confound it, he was acting like Charity Dinsmore. But he thought this inner pain might never go away. He wanted her to tell him it would. It had to.

She waited until he sat down again. "That is because you can only see your hurt at the moment." She held up her hand to stop his protests. "And I certainly understand that. But you must allow me my own feelings, as well. I love you more than life itself, you know that. But when you have let go of your blinding anger, I think you will find that Kathryn is not your enemy, either.

"Son, my heart breaks for you both. I do not side with her, or you for that matter. I only want you to see there *are* two sides."

"I am glad you can forgive her so easily. But somehow I doubt you will forgive her enough to align her sullied name with ours."

"Christopher!"

He walked away toward the drawing room doors. "I must attend to some estate business. I will be in my study for a few hours."

"Son, wait."

He stopped but did not turn around.

"Is this what happened when Kathryn tried to explain her decisions and actions to you?"

He did not move a muscle.

"I see, you never let her get past the point of *your* pride. You did not wait to see if she asked for or deserved your forgiveness." She got up and walked around him so they were face-to-face. "Christopher, be the loving, forgiving man that you are. Do not turn into a bitter, unhappy man. *'And be ye kind one to another, tenderhearted, forgiving one another...'"*

She put her hands on his arms. "My dear, we will never know why God led Kathryn through such trials at so early an age. But we must believe that it was He who kept her safe throughout the toughest of circumstances. We can be sure she will have gained experience she will use for the rest of her life. Someone will just have to help her see that it is *because* of His unconditional love that she lived through it. Don't you see? The odds of the two of you being reunited in such a way shows you, and the others who know you, that God's will *can* be accomplished even though we make such mistakes in life. Eventually, as now, He will make these things clear to us. Go to God and ask Him to help you deal with this blow. You know He will do it."

"I know she *eloped*," he said, the last word spoken in disgust. "Apparently you are more tolerant than the rest of the *ton*."

"As are you! Christopher, I have never heard you judge another, yet here you sit condemning a woman you cared for without the benefit of a trial. We cannot judge others based on our standards. God's standards are all that matters, and He *does* know the whole story."

Dalton had expected to spend several days there, but he had also expected his mother to be on his side. He came back to London directly after meeting with his steward. His mother's goodbye included a petition that he not become a bitter and judgmental man.

It was too late for that. He *was* bitter. He had lived with a heart torn in two since she left him nine years ago, and he blamed her for the difficulty he had in trusting any other woman. He had never felt the depth of love for another since.

He got up and poured himself a brandy at the side bar. He walked to the mantel, leaning his head on his arm as he stared into the fire. He saw her face there, beautiful, kind, witty and…loving. He splashed brandy as he slammed the glass down and walked away from the fire. Seeing her face only made him angry again.

He could not move on with his life as if nothing had happened. He would ask God's help, but he knew what was left of his heart must be protected.

She had spoken of things he did not understand, and with his head still in a fog he remembered little of it. But he knew enough that she had faced some horrid things that made her angry at him. He had left there completely and utterly confused and hurt. But now *he* was angry.

He knew what he must do. He would go back to Dinsmore Manor to purchase his horseflesh. And he would make sure she understood how she had hurt him…for the second time. He would show her that he was better off without her.

A little voice in his head said, *"Vengeance is Mine, saith the Lord,"* but he planned no revenge, though some might see it that way. His conscience was clear and his actions were necessary.

He took his stairs two at a time, calling his man to prepare him for a fortnight away from London.

Kathryn thought she had lived through the worst pain life could deal out. She now knew she had not.

It had been two weeks since that night, and she had not slept at all. Each time she closed her eyes, the scene under the tree would play over and over on the inside of her eyelids. And it was not the attack she kept reliving. It was the awful scene afterward with Lord Dalton.

She had no idea how he intended to use the information he had discovered that night; he could have gone to Lady Dinsmore and told her she had an imposter living under her roof. He could have gone back to Town, and all of London would know he had discovered her whereabouts and she had sunk beneath reproach. He did neither.

But the anguish of that night would not let go of her. She did not think she could have helped what happened. She was terrified and angry after being accosted by Jack Dawkins. She was in no state of mind to remember to keep her hood on.

No, she could not lie, at least not to herself. She could have stayed in her bedroom and never gone to the bridge at all. She was so tired of thinking of it all the time.

So tired that thoughts of him would not disappear.

So Kathryn faltered in astonishment when she saw him walk through the nursery door. Had she conjured him up? No, it was him.

The children's exuberance covered her embarrassment. What was he doing here? She felt so foolish in her wig and glasses because he knew she hid behind them. Could he feel her pain despite her unemotional recounting of the past nine years? Dare she hope he had come back to see her?

"Lord Dalton, Lord Dalton," the children chimed as they both hurried toward the elegantly dressed man. "You have come back! And you have come to visit us in the nursery. That is a great treat, is it not, Miss Montgomery? No one but you has ever come to visit us."

She must act normally in front of the children. "Indeed it is. Perhaps you should show your appreciation with a proper curtsy and bow." Everything came out stilted. She must be calm until she knew why he was back. Her smile belied any severity to Lacey and Jacob, and the children proceeded to rectify their initial behavior with a race to present a teetering curtsy and an elegant leg to impress the earl.

Kathryn took the time to covertly study the man before her. *Elegant* was a completely unsatisfactory description of his appearance. Even in buckskins and top boots he was every inch the gentleman, and she thought him even more handsome.

"Ah, *Miss Montgomery,* I hoped to find you here, as well. I thought I heard from Lady Dinsmore that you have been unwell."

Her heart finally slowed to a steady beat. "I assure you that I am very well, I thank you." She did not know if his intention had been true, but he seemed…different.

"I find, *Miss Montgomery,* that I owe you an apology, though the offense has not yet occurred."

Kathryn no longer doubted his intentions. By the second *Miss Montgomery,* she knew he had not forgiven her. Then why was he here at all? "That is a very strange apology, my lord. Perhaps if you tell me what the offense may be, we will find no apology to be necessary."

Those devastating dimples peeped out as he tousled the children's hair. "I am afraid there is no way to stop it. I did try. I told them I did not wish to be a burden, but they were quite adamant."

"I am afraid I do not understand you, my lord."

"I believe Lady Dinsmore and Miss Charity are planning a dinner party in my honor."

"That is a surprise, my lord, but it is not an of-fense…" She studied him with wary eyes. "I did not know you had returned, yet there has been time to plan a party?"

"Oh, no, the party was planned before. It just had to be postponed. No, even though they advise me you will be arranging it, I was told you will not be needed to make up the numbers at dinner that night. I am very sorry."

The smug look on Lord Dalton's face made her angry, and he knew it. Why had he come back? Of course, Charity would want to flaunt her captive to all of Trotton, but if it had been planned before he left, he would be well out of it by staying away.

The two were brought back to the notice of the chil-dren by Lacey. She was shyly tugging at his coattails. "Lord Dalton," she said, "may I show you my draw-ing?"

Kathryn was relieved he had not changed toward the children. He sat, quite informally on a chair one foot high, and graciously accepted the large parchment with due respect. He studied it for several moments then stated, "I do believe it is an exact replica of the lovely gazebo down by the lake. Am I correct?"

Lacey beamed over her shoulder at her, then turned the sweetest smile upon his lordship.

"I believe this patch of trees may even boast the fox's den I noticed when I rode by this morning. Have you seen the family, then?"

Lacey lost her poise, and Kathryn was sure she was going to burst into tears.

"My lord," Kathryn explained, "we are not yet certain that Sir John is aware of the partially hidden den. But as we have certainly seen them, we wished to keep their presence concealed quite as long as possible." She smiled at Lacey, giving her a mental nudge.

"I did not realize my drawing gave them away so clearly. Pray do not tell Papa, my lord. Miss Montgomery has explained why we should not tell fibs to our family, but she thinks not pointing them out would protect the babies until they can look after themselves. We would never outright tell a lie, sir."

Kathryn saw a scowl on Lord Dalton's face. "And you learned that from Miss Montgomery? How interesting." He finally looked at her, his face angled as if he was surprised, indeed.

He returned his attention to the children, and she closed her eyes. She still did not know for sure why he was back, but he made it clear he would torment her while his stay lasted.

What if he planned to tell Sir John that she was a fraud? She would lose her position, her income…and the children. Was he that angry? He knew she was living a lie, and he would make sure she was still living with the consequences of her actions.

But why must the consequences of her mistake in judgment be upon her for the rest of her life? She had confessed over and over, but she found no forgiveness—not from God, not from anyone. Lord Dalton certainly had not forgiven her; deep in her heart she had always known how it would be. Lacey's voice brought her back to the present. "Oh, thank you, sir. May I go work on it some more before our lessons are to start?"

"By all means, child. I will hope to see it in a few days, when I can only imagine it will be a masterpiece!"

"Lord Dalting, Lord Dalting," cried the little boy, now eye to eye with him and mangling his name in the same double opening as his father. Lord Dalton's spontaneous laughter brought a smile to the face of the shy nurse in the rocking chair by the window. Kathryn was so thankful he would not hurt the children because of her.

"I understand, Master Jacob, that you have been working on a great surprise. I have been waiting for an opportunity to see it."

The elation on the boy's face spoke volumes. "Would you like to see it now, sir?"

"Yes, if I may." Suddenly an obvious fear gripped the child, and with only the innocence a little one could produce, his face fell as he asked, "Miss Montgomery, do you think he will be dis'pointed? I mean, not know what it is…will that ruin the surprise?"

Kathryn rose and walked to the small boy, and Lord Dalton and Lacey followed behind. "Jacob, it is a marvelous wonder, you must not doubt it." She took his hand and was leading the small band to a room set off to the side of the nursery.

As they entered the room, she and Jacob quietly moved off to the left, leaving a clear view of a cardboard tower standing in the center of the room, quite as high as Jacob himself. There was one moment of silence.

"Why, it is a Martello Tower! Which one is it, lad?"

Dalton's question produced a gasp from the nurse behind him, but Kathryn had every expectation of his recognizing the small version of the edifices that dotted the coastline of Sussex. He did not disappoint Jacob.

"Miss Montgomery, Miss Montgomery, he knows, he knows!" beamed the boy, now in perfect double rhythm. "All of the footmen think it is just a castle, but Lord Dalting knows it is a Martello Tower!"

"Lord Dalton, dear," she softly corrected him, "and yes, it is truly gratifying. Now he asked *you* a question, and may have others, so you must show it to him more closely. We are all very proud of your hard work, and you must satisfy his curiosity since he has been so smart as to recognize it."

Kathryn transferred the boy's hand from hers to Lord Dalton's, and let Jacob lead him to the patchwork structure. Lord Dalton bent to one knee to be on the same level as his instructor.

"I do not know what number it is, sir. I forgot that. But it is the one below Chichester. Miss Montgomery has seen several in Lewes near where she grew up and in Brighton…did you know the one in Seaford has a real moat around it?" Once started, his excitement grew and he could not talk fast enough. "Miss Montgomery took us to see it on her day off from Charity." He looked directly into Lord Dalton's eyes and asked the question burning in his mind. "How do *you* know about the towers, sir?"

Dalton sank to the floor to inspect Jacob's project from a closer vantage point. "My home is in Rye, Jacob.

Do you know where that is?" At the shake of the boy's head, he continued. "It, too, is in Sussex. In any event, Rye has *two* Martello Towers, and I must claim myself as excited by them as you seem to be. You are quite the expert!"

Kathryn could see the exhilaration on Lord Dalton's face at pleasing Jacob. She just wanted to slip away. How could he be so charming one moment and so cruel the next? Perhaps it would be better if she told Lady Dinsmore and be done with it.

"I always thought there should be more than one cannon in each tower myself, and I appreciate your greater effort to protect England's shores."

She could tell that Lord Dalton was now enjoying himself immensely. He addressed the boy again. "Suppose you and I were to add a moat to this great creation?"

Jacob's screech of delight surprised Lord Dalton, and he laughed heartily.

"May we, Miss Montgomery? May we please? That would be splendid, sir!"

She watched the smile disappear as they turned to her expectantly. They must see no change in her, so she pretended sternness.

"Very well, minx. If Nurse agrees, you may attempt to build your moat. But there are conditions. First, you must get your father's permission to importune his guest, and you must promise to be completely satisfied with whatever amount of time Lord Dalton may spare for you. Finally," she said, growing very serious, "you must *promise* there will be no real water!"

Lacey started to giggle, and within moments Jacob and Lord Dalton laughed, teasing Jacob about flooding the nursery. The noisy clearing of a starched-up throat interrupted their joy, and all heads turned to see a very stern Jarvis standing in the doorway. He made no particular comment about earls sitting cross-legged upon the nursery floor; however, his expression clearly showed his thoughts on the matter.

"Lord Dalton, Sir John has asked me to inform you that he has been waiting for you in the stables this half hour or more."

"Please tell Sir John I will attend him directly. I will fetch my gloves and join him in the stables."

"As you wish, my lord."

"Well, my friends, it seems I must say farewell for the nonce. I thank you for an agreeable morning, and perhaps we may enjoy the pleasure again before I leave Trotton." He bowed quite regally to both children, then turned to Kathryn. "Please forgive my intrusion into your own time with the children," he said formally while bowing. She curtsied in deference.

"Your servant, ma'am."

Kathryn flinched at the coldness in his voice. She was so thankful he remained kind to the children, but if his primary intention was to hurt her, he had succeeded. Her hope that his stay would be a short one died as she thought about the party to be given in his honor and the promise to Jacob of building a moat. Would the consequences never end?

She had spent the past nine years regretting the loss of his love. Apparently, God did not think that was long enough.

Chapter Eight

"I vow, Papa, if I hear one more word about your hideous hunters, I shall die of boredom." Charity rapped her fan across her father's arm as she laughingly said the words, but made it clear to all in the room that she was bringing the subject of horses to a close.

They were assembled in the gold salon for tea, and it was evident from the moment they gathered there that Charity was bursting for attention. Unfortunately, several interruptions by other members of her family only fed her frustration.

It began when Nurse entered the room with the children. Their jubilant excitement when they caught sight of the earl caused them to forget propriety and run to him, all legs and words.

"Bless my soul, children," began Lady Dinsmore, "what can you be about, accosting his lordship in this manner? Do calm yourselves at once."

"You must not scold them, Lady Dinsmore," Lord Dalton quickly entreated. "I fear I brought this on myself and had no idea I should be the cause of disrupting your tea. It is I who should be apologizing, I assure you."

"Oh, Lord Dalton, you must be all about in your head," said Charity, waving away his words. "In what way could *you* possibly be responsible for this unruly conduct?"

Kathryn determined that Lord Dalton should not draw fire upon himself, and interceded in his defense. "Charity, His Lordship has done nothing to warrant the blame. In that you are correct. He was kind enough to visit the children in the nursery this morning, and they have quite adopted him." She smiled slightly as she lowered her voice, addressing Lady Dinsmore. "I should have warned them that their manners in the nursery have no bearing on their manners during tea."

Sir John choked on a scone. "The devil you say! Is it for these ragamuffins you kept me waiting in the stables this morning?" After swallowing a gulp of brandy to clear his throat, he slapped his thigh and laughed. "If that don't beat the Dutch!"

Jacob, understanding his father's jovial mood, decided it was the perfect time to put forth his request, and ran to stand beside his father's chair.

"Papa, Papa, I have a mo…ment…tous favor to ask," he said, looking at Lord Dalton for approval. His Lordship and Kathryn chuckled at the same time, and Dalton quickly looked away from her.

Fortunately, Jacob barely drew breath. "Papa, Lord Darton offered to help me build a moat for my Martello Tower. Can he, please, oh, please, Papa?"

Sir John looked even more perplexed than before. He cleared his throat, not certain why his guest would wish to spend a morning entertaining his youngest child but not about to question it. "Of course, my boy," he addressed Lord Dalton. "We told you we were as informal as you like. But you must not allow little Jakey to make a pest of himself, what?"

"Little Jakey" took umbrage at both the nickname and the accusation. "I already promised Lord Danton I would do most of the work myself," he said in a dejected voice.

"Indeed, Sir John, Master Jacob is not a pest, and it was I who offered. I have a fondness for children, and it will be no hardship, I assure you."

That was the point at which Charity became tired of being ignored.

"Darling," her mother chimed in for the first time, "why not let Miss Montgomery take the children their tea, then we may talk of the party."

Kathryn reminded herself that this was supposed to be a surprise to her. "A party?" she said, knowing it would go a long way to keeping Charity happy. She herself was having a hard time staying in the same room as Dalton. She did not think she would survive his coldness.

"My dear, you were not with us when we discussed this with Lord Dalton when he was here before. We are to have a small dinner party for his entertainment." Lady Dinsmore smiled at her daughter as she spoke.

As Kathryn already knew, she was to be called into service for this and began making a mental list of the items such an endeavor would entail. Charity would be of little help, and Lady Dinsmore just barely managed to keep control of the household routine. But she found she did not mind. It would be a change in her normally mundane disagreements with Charity, and she would remain too busy to be hurt by Lord Dalton's arrows.

"When is this party to be?"

"We have not as yet set the date, but may we do so now, Mama?"

Lady Dinsmore appeared quite content with her daughter's congenial behavior. "That is a splendid idea, my dear. While we are all gathered, we may decide on the perfect time. I suggest we have it a week from today. His Lordship will only be here another week or so, and I believe the Farnhams are leaving for Brighton sometime in the next fortnight."

"But Mama, shall we have enough time to get the invitations out? It will not be very much notice. Perhaps we should wait the full ten days."

Kathryn could read Charity like a book. She assumed putting it off would give her more time to bring Lord Dalton up to scratch. She could see the machinations in Charity's mind all too clearly. What a boon it would be if she could make it an engagement party!

"I hate to be a fly in the ointment," Dalton said contritely, "but I do not know that I will be here much more than a week. I have almost decided which horses will suit me, and there are few left to test." When the sound of someone loudly clearing his throat reached his ears, he smiled. "Of course, there is also the matter of a certain moat we discussed earlier." He became serious again. "If it would not be too much trouble, a week from tomorrow would be quite amenable for me."

"It is settled, then," Lady Dinsmore said at the same time Charity whined, "but the invitations."

Kathryn knew her cue. "Charity, I will write them out this afternoon, and they may be delivered tomorrow."

"Of course!" she exclaimed. "It will give you something to occupy your time while I entertain Lord Dalton."

Kathryn put a smile on her face and reminded herself that what the girl said was true. It would always be someone else's place to entertain Lord Dalton, especially now.

No, this was not right at all. He was not sure exactly what he was expecting, but it was not her docile acceptance. It only made him feel mean. He wanted her to know how *he* felt. She had left him shattered nine years ago. She had played him for a fool by running off with Salford. And she had not told him who she was during his first stay. He wanted her to feel the pain he felt, not go into a protective shell that kept his uncharacteristic barbs at bay.

Worse, this was all making him feel guilty. He had nothing to feel guilty about! At least that's what he kept telling himself. He knew it was ungentlemanly, but did she not deserve a small upbraiding? Each time he purposely said hurtful words, God pricked his heart. But he ignored the prodding and waited for the next opportunity. He hoped it would give him more pleasure than it had thus far.

His thoughts turned back to the present conversation, and he watched as the sly minx treated her companion as a servant. She gave no thought to Kathryn's feelings. Perhaps Charity would succeed where he did not. Perhaps he *and* Charity together would bring about the desired reaction!

"I must beg leave to help, Miss Charity." He spoke to her in a sweet tone of voice he had never used before. "Is there not some way in which a male may be useful in these circumstances?" He knew his offer to be unusual, but he doubted anyone other than Kathryn would notice. More the better.

"La, my lord. You love to tease me." The girl's flagrant flirting had brought about a reaction from the wrong person! "You must not trouble yourself in the least." She placed her hand on his arm and looked up at him with adoring eyes. "But you are a dear to offer."

Dalton was suddenly struck by the seriousness of the situation in which he now found himself. This was no schoolgirl flirtation; the child was trying to trap him into marriage! Had he been invited here for that purpose? No, he could not believe Sir John to be such a schemer. The chit was definitely getting help from her mother. He saw it clearly now, but had it actually been a plan? He could only hope it had been conceived after his arrival.

He must be on his guard in the future. He had no intention of being leg-shackled to a spoiled brat. No, he decided he could not risk using the chit to irritate Kathryn. Dalton suddenly transferred his gaze to her companion, praying he saw no duplicity there. He needed to see her eyes; he would detect the truth there. No! He would not believe it of her, despite their current contretemps.

He knew what he must do. He would keep Kathryn and the children as close to him as possible. It would not be difficult; they were already at tea every day, and she joined them each night for dinner. It would still allow him the opportunity to avenge himself on Kathryn, but would protect him from the grasping daughter of the house. He could not imagine a fate worse than being married to a spoiled, coddled child who thought her beauty gave her the right to ride roughshod over others.

"My lord—" the sugary voice was much too close to his ear "—there *is* one way you could be of assistance, though I hope it is not a task too onerous." Her eyelashes fluttered, and he walked to the tea tray to set down his cup and to put a room's distance between them.

"In what way, Miss Charity?" he questioned, trying for the perfect balance of aloofness and interest.

The girl did not even seem to notice. "Perhaps tomorrow we could go on that drive we have had to put off since you were called away. I could show you the countryside, and we could deliver the invitations as we went. Why, we could take a picnic and make an afternoon of it!"

Lady Dinsmore turned to Kathryn. "Kate, dear, perhaps you would consent to chaperone Charity with Lord Dalton tomorrow?" He silently thanked the matron, though she was not aware of it. Kathryn would be no threat to Charity, but if he were any judge, she could put a damper on the girl's outrageous conduct and make her quite uncomfortable in his presence.

Dalton would get her to join them if he had to move heaven and earth to do so.

"Your mother is quite right, Miss Charity. Running the horses, I have seen little of the actual farms or the people on your grounds. I would be delighted at the prospect."

"But we are not visiting the tenants, my lord. We need to deliver the invitations. They will not be included."

Even Dalton understood Charity's real concern. She wanted to deliver the invitations so all of her friends could see her accompanied by an earl. The more envious she could make them, the better. Well, he had little interest in seeing either, so he would let them decide.

Kathryn interrupted, apparently to stop the girl's whining. "Charity, I will write the invitations this evening, and James may deliver them first thing in the morning. You will then be able to decide which path you will choose on the morrow."

"Of course, I do not know why I did not think of that myself. And if we are to visit my friends, Kate need not join us. I will be perfectly chaperoned at each stop."

Oh, no, that was not part of his plan. What about in between houses? He turned to address Kathryn. "I would be delighted, as well, to have *Miss Montgomery's* company."

Charity would no doubt berate her mother roundly.

* * *

In the end, Charity was more than happy with the arrangements that surrounded their outing. At quite the exact moment they were to set off, none other than the Farnham brothers appeared, accompanied by their sister, Cynthia, as well as Mr. Bolton, Charity's most fervent suitor. Charity clapped in delight at the thought of her friends receiving a preview of *her* lord.

"Mama, we must still be sure one of the footmen is able to deliver the invitations today. And we shall go to Easebourne Priory for our picnic!"

"Miss Montgomery?" Lady Dinsmore asked as Kathryn removed her bonnet. "Where do you suppose you are off to?"

"Lady Dinsmore, this outing certainly does not require a chaperone!"

"Of course not, my dear. But *you* will be more necessary on this picnic than before! Indeed, you know more about the Priory in your four months with us than these children know from living near it since birth. Put your bonnet back on, and do not let me hear one word of protest." Her harshness was in jest, as her real affection for Kathryn allowed that she deserved a treat as much as anyone. Kathryn knew, however, that while another pair of watchful eyes was Lady Dinsmore's goal, Lord Dalton had a few of his own.

Though at one time she would have been quite happy just being in Lord Dalton's company, she now knew a day with Lacey and Jacob in the nursery would have been preferable.

Having arrived at the Priory only a few hours later,

Lord Dalton was still castigating her for her actions of long ago. "I quite appreciate your tour of the ruins, *Miss Montgomery*," Lord Dalton said, instinctively placing a hand at her back over a patch of rough ground, then, realizing what he had done, removed his hand as if it had been burned. "I daresay it is not the way you intended to spend your day."

They had arrived at Easebourne in varying stages of frustration, but glad to see that the servants had indeed arrived before them and had set up an alfresco banquet grand enough to impress the Regent himself.

After being cooped up, talked to death and choked by dust, all were happy to relax in the shade and indulge in cold chicken, pigeon pies, cheese, fruit and tangy lemonade in one large group. Charity had been counting on lunch solely with Lord Dalton. She had openly shown her pique and, after the repast, had suggested they get on with the tour.

Kathryn could see that Charity was put out as she looked at the earl coyly and put her hand in the crook of his arm. It seemed Lord Dalton knew Charity's intent, as he blatantly invited her companion along as the expert amongst them.

Charity, now openly disgruntled, removed her arm from Lord Dalton's and placed it in the crook of Kathryn's. Apparently she was not happy, but not disgusted enough to leave him alone with her companion.

Kathryn was determined to be pleasant and amiable once they were thrown together. She knew he was happy that she was uncomfortable, especially while covered in her loathsome disguise, but she would allow him his revenge. She deserved it.

"Indeed, I will sink very low in your opinion and admit I love this tumbled-down old building. I love to bring the children here. To own the truth, I think they have begun to believe they are being punished for crimes unknown when we come. Would you not agree, Charity?"

Lord Dalton pretended no notice of Kathryn. "Miss Charity, the study of old architecture is one of my passions. Do you share it?" They sat down upon a pile of fallen stones, and Kathryn leaned back against the remaining wall. Charity did not share it, but she would certainly take advantage of it.

"Of course, my lord. Easebourne Priory has been my friend since childhood."

Had things been quite different, the old Lord Dalton would have shared a private smile over such a lie.

Instead, Kathryn spoke in platitudes. "I like to spend my time off with Lacey and Jacob, and though they both love to read, we gather such vivid information from actual visits." She smiled a little to herself. "So I kill two birds with one stone."

Charity was quickly becoming bored, and Kathryn could not be alone with Lord Dalton. "I'm sure Charity and I would like to hear about your travels, my lord. I always hated the nonchalant discussions of war in London, when anyone with a brain must realize the dreadful nature of it all." She sighed.

"Oh, yes, my lord, do tell me about your regimentals. I so adore a man in regimentals!"

Only a few weeks ago, he would have looked at Kathryn in complete understanding of Charity's childish remark. Now he seemed bent on pleasing her. Perhaps he truly *had* decided on her for a wife. If that were so, then she was well out of it.

"Ah, they are quite handsome, I assure you, Miss Charity." Kathryn heard him say under his breath, "Especially once they have bullet holes and saber slits in them." Oh, what he must have seen in times of battle.

It seemed Charity had heard him, as well. But she laughed. "My lord, you do love to tease me. Of course they would not be handsome then. Why, I assumed you had several pairs in the event your colonel had a party. I have heard there are great balls in between battles."

Neither of them could respond to such a comment.

Suddenly, Lord Dalton turned to her. "*Miss Montgomery,*" he said with emphasis, "I still have not heard about your London Season." Apparently trying to flirt with Charity did not give him enough pleasure.

"My come-out was many years ago. But as I have mentioned, it was not a successful one, and I am afraid I have no taste for London any longer."

Charity tittered. "Can you imagine, my lord? She does not like London!"

Ignoring her, he persisted in his inquiry of Kathryn. "But you must have learned all you could while you were in Town?" He smiled as if speaking to a stranger. "Despite your distaste for the place, you must own it has much to offer in the way of stimulating one's mind."

She could remind him that the social whirl allowed her little time for more intellectual pursuits, but she watched her words more closely now and would give him nothing more to pierce her heart. "Unfortunately, my visit was cut short and I was not there long enough to see many of London's famous sights. That is only one of the regrets I have about my Season." Why had she added that? Oh, her wretched tongue!

"Too solemn, by half, ma'am. Miss Charity, have you perhaps visited London?"

Charity proceeded to monopolize him with quite a monologue. No, she had not been to Town, but she had been to Bath. She needed neither of them as she spoke without ceasing, but she kept tugging at Lord Dalton's sleeve to be sure he was listening to her.

Kathryn knew he was sorry he had asked for Charity's opinion when he turned once more to her. "I do not know much about your lot in life. What brought you to your present occupation?"

She flinched at the hurtful words. "If you two will excuse me, I am the chaperone on this outing. I will go see to the others." She curtsied and walked away. She did not even bother with her shuffle; she was so hurt she did not care. And she did not give a hang about leaving her charge alone with Lord Dalton. Indeed, she hoped they would be very happy together.

"No, ma'am, I am not asking for information. I wished to make an observation, but it may not apply in your case." His voice grew fainter as she got farther away. Before this week she would have taken that as an apology.

She noticed by the time she reached the others that the couple was not far behind. She supposed he did not want Kathryn to miss even one moment of their burgeoning love.

"Oh, yes, Lord Dalton, I adore strawberries," was all she heard before she sat down with Cynthia Farnham.

When they all had their fill of dessert, Kathryn watched him charm the group of children with war stories and horse races and exploits she knew had never happened. But she had the feeling he was somehow trying to make up for his earlier comment, taking on the duty of keeping the group occupied and carefree.

She knew his hurtful words to her came out of his own pain, but there was nothing she could do about it now. He had even used Charity to protect him from being alone with her. If he would just speak his mind, let all of his anger out, she knew he would be able to go on with his life and put their tiny space of time in the past to rest. She had given up on him long ago, and she had no more right to him. She'd hoped that someday they could work it out, perhaps remain friends, but she knew it was too late for that now. So she would let him punish her as long as he wished, then she would watch him leave her, glad to be out of it. At this point all she could hope for was that she would not lose her position through him.

Unfortunately, Charity had had enough of Mr. Bolton, after the attentions of the earl. "Lord Dalton, you must be bored to tears with these children. I will rescue you." She sat closer to him and touched his arm. "You see, I know you are too honorable to interrupt them." She put her hand through the crook of his arm, giving him no choice but to stand up.

He quickly removed it once standing. "I do not think we should leave full responsibility for the group to Miss Montgomery. We must not be selfish."

"Oh, my lord, that is why Kate is here. She will keep a watchful eye, do not doubt it." She turned her brilliant green eyes to his in adoration. He laughed out loud and patted her arm. "As the male, I think I would keep them in line much better. Will you not sit back down?"

"No, I will not." She yelled for a servant, making all on the blanket jump in surprise. "I believe we should return home. Pack all of this up, now!" No one would gainsay Charity, so they did as she wished.

Kathryn had heard his laughter only moments ago with Charity, and she found herself very close to tears. They had shared laughter easily years ago, and even here, before he knew who she really was. She thought if she had many more days like this, she could easily fall out of love with the Lord Dalton of London days.

And without that, she would shrivel up and die inside.

Chapter Nine

The next day Kathryn avoided Lord Dalton any way she could. Fortunately, the work on the party became increasingly more taxing and could always be used as an excuse. How he filled his time, she did not know.

Had she been able to go to the bridge, to be free just for an hour, she would have gone. But Lord Dalton was so angry at her, she would not be in the least surprised if he actually went every night in the hopes of another opportunity to pull her down.

Instead, she ensconced herself in the large dining room, where the party would move after dinner. The affair had increased significantly in size over a few days, and had now turned into a full-blown ball. Or as much of a ball as you could have with fewer than thirty people. No one ever used that word, but that is what it had become.

Kathryn had been called upon to pick a theme and order the decorations accordingly. She had been thinking of the many balls she had attended in London, look-ing for one memorable enough to help her decide.

Suddenly, she remembered. There was only one event that she could recall in minute detail, and it had not been a ball at all. It had been a night at Vauxhall Gardens.

Lord Dalton had asked her father's permission to take her, as both men knew there was much that went on there that was not suitable for a young girl. But he had promised to make up his own party of guests and rent one of the private boxes so they would all be safely situated there. He even guaranteed her father that his parents would be with them, as well.

Kathryn remembered it now as one of the most amazing nights of her life.

When Dalton told her they were to go, she had hugged him with pleasure. He had been startled, but she remembered he certainly returned it. They both pretended it had not happened. She knew her father would not let her go in the care of anyone other than Lord Dalton, and she did not wish to experience it with anyone else.

He had picked her up in full evening wear, and his handsomeness nearly took her breath away. She some-times wondered if her bearing and taste in clothes could live up to his standard, but either way she thanked God for him. She began to love him in earnest.

His parents were in Town, and with the two other couples Lord Dalton had chosen, she was so very ex-cited.

They had to take a barge on the Thames River to get

there, and it was all so new and exciting. They arrived to twinkling lights strung throughout the trees, a private box with wonderful food and music that filled the air.

"May I have this dance, Lady Kathryn?" She heard the strains of the waltz, and she gave him a dazzling smile.

"You may, Lord Dalton."

She excused herself to his mother, and walked on his arm to the dance floor. Between the lights and the stars above, everything seemed to sparkle.

"Are you having a good time, my sweet?"

"Must you even ask? It is magical."

"I believe it is only magical when you are here with the right person." He looked into her eyes as they danced. *"I find it quite magical myself."*

She blushed at the compliment, and could not stop smiling.

"I think your mother very dear, Dalton."

"She is that, and I am so glad you like her. Actually, coming here was her idea. It seems she and my father came two years ago and thought it a romantic night."

"I think I would agree with that, sir."

"So formal! I liked the sound of Dalton upon your lips better."

"Then I will not abuse it, my lord. It might become too commonplace."

"Never. Not when it is you using it."

At that moment, fireworks burst into the night sky, and she was totally spellbound. "Oh, Dalton!"

They continued their dance in silence, both lost in

their own thoughts, but both knowing they thought of the same things.

When he led her back to the box, his mother sat alone. "All by yourself?"

He raised her hand and kissed it. "Where is Father?"

She laughed. "He went to get me a little more of the shaved ham this half hour or more. I suspect he met one of his old cronies and they are toasting the old days. Would you be a dear and bring me your father or the ham, whichever you find sooner?"

He laughed as he left, and Kathryn remembered being nervous alone with her. "I can see where Lord Dalton gets his sense of humor," she said shyly. "I understand it was your idea to come here tonight, my lady. I am so glad. It is a wonderful place!"

"It has its dark side, my dear, but for the most part I find it wonderful myself." She pulled out the chair next to her and indicated Kathryn should sit by her.

"Christopher is quite enchanted with you, my dear. I believe it cannot have escaped your notice."

She blushed. "I do not know why he should be. There are so many wonderful girls out this year." She looked down at her lap. "But I am glad he has bestowed so much of his time on me."

His mother put a finger under her chin to lift her face. "You need not be embarrassed, my child. Though still a young man, he has always known his own mind and I am very proud of him."

"You should be, ma'am. I am sure his thoughtfulness is a testimony to you and Lord Dalton. He gives

you credit all the time. I lost my mother when I was young, so my father has been both to me, but I miss her every day." She swiped at a tear. *"But I am glad to finally meet you."*

"Very prettily said, my dear. I have been looking forward to that pleasure, as well."

Sometimes that night invaded her dreams, and she would wake up in the morning thinking it had only happened last night. Then her stark room would take its place, and she knew it had only been a dream. Sometimes she thought that whole Season was a dream—a dream that ultimately turned into a nightmare.

Well, she would decorate the dining room like a starry night. She would never call it a night at Vauxhall, or he would know she still thought of it. But she would get pleasure out of recreating that night, no matter how long, or how many mistakes, ago.

Dalton was frustrated. He had virtually no time alone with Kathryn, so had little chance of continuing her purgatory. It was her just due. Was it not? He *had* hurt her at the Priory that day, and he was immediately sorry.

He watched her constantly, whether with her or from a distance. He was astounded at her beauty, even beneath that ridiculous disguise. Her face was still her face; it was obvious despite not seeing her eyes. He berated himself over and over for letting her mask fool him.

She took no time for herself. If she was not dancing to Charity's tune, she was volunteering to run an errand for Lady Dinsmore or playing with the children in the nursery. He could admit that in that way, she had not changed. He was beginning to lose sight of whatever goal he'd had.

He would not give up the fight yet. He had a plan for dinner that night. He had not quite determined what he expected to accomplish with it. Did he want to embarrass her? Did he want to see her squirm? Did he want her to hurt as she hurt him? He wasn't sure anymore.

He could feel anger beginning to fade. It was not in his normal personality, and he was starting to feel as badly about himself as he was making her feel. But he would go ahead with this one last reminder, then he would go home more at peace. *Dear Lord, all I want is some peace. Only You know how she hurt me.* And his conscience was pricked at the thought that God also knew this was not the right way to go about it.

But he patiently bided his time at dinner, waiting for the opening in the conversation he both feared and anticipated. There was little time left before he would be leaving and, as yet, his hurt had yet to be assuaged. Would it ever be?

He had lain awake the previous night, punching his pillow, needing a culprit of some kind, but he found no release in the exercise. His mind would not let it go. He must determine what to do about Kathryn. He must decide whether his dogged pursuit of justice should cease. His mother would tell him to pray about it and let God take care of the rest. And he had been praying about it. He apparently felt as if God could not work in the time constraints he was under. So he decided to help Him.

So Dalton sat at the Dinsmore dining table, avoiding veiled hints from the green-eyed she-devil next to him. He tried concentrating on the horse his host was in raptures over, but was also listening to Kathryn discuss party preparations with Lady Dinsmore.

His patience ran out, however, and he determined to mete out her punishment to a captive audience.

The moment finally came as the footmen cleared away the last course and began to serve dessert—raspberries in clotted cream. All conversation stopped for the moment, and he seized his opportunity.

He cleared his throat, catching the attention of the small group around him, and he nonchalantly said, "I have remembered something today which I have been meaning to ask of you. I happened upon a strange event the day after I arrived in Trotton. There was a woman being accosted on the bridge over the Rother River. Though she routed him, and assured me she was not hurt, I was hoping one of you could verify that the woman suffered no lasting injuries."

The angered look of the daughter of the house and the clatter of Kathryn's spoon on Lady Dinsmore's fine china were the only responses he received.

"A woman, you say? A woman…? We must have more information to go on than that, my boy. Attacked, you say? Why did you not mention this sooner?"

"I beg your pardon, Sir John," said Lord Dalton. "I was called away the next day. And I did not mean to startle Miss Montgomery so. My apologies."

Charity, however, remarked acidly, "Perhaps you

can describe this paragon that has so occupied your thoughts."

His frustration showed in his words. "I did not say she was a paragon, Miss Charity. And I assure you it was only concern for the safety of one of your neighbors that I asked."

"Perhaps, my lord," Kathryn said, without looking at him, "you could give us a little more information. Crime is not a common word in Trotton."

"Ah, *Miss Montgomery,*" replied Lord Dalton, "a cool head as always."

"You see, Sir John, on one of my first nights here, I was unable to sleep and decided a walk in the night air might be just the thing. Having already crossed the bridge when I first arrived, I was interested in seeing it upon closer inspection. I thought the walk long enough to help me sleep."

He watched Kathryn in complete frustration. It seemed she would not be put out of countenance no matter what he did. He almost admired that. She obviously knew what he was doing. Was she trying to protect *this* family?

"At first I assumed it was a tête-à-tête between two locals, but I soon knew otherwise when I saw the man held his prey at knifepoint. Realizing her danger, I raced to help. However, my presence was enough to prevent any real damage, and the attacker ran off."

He had told the truth, somewhat, but had left out so many of the details that it was hardly recognizable as one of the most dreadful nights of his life. He had discovered his first love—the love that had left him bereft nine years ago—masquerading as someone else.

Evidently, Charity wondered the same thing. "My lord, are you saying we have a criminal among us and you said nothing of it before?"

"Miss Charity, please believe that had I thought any danger remained, I certainly should have presented it to your father sooner. I felt sure in the knowledge that the attacker would not tarry long in the vicinity, having had two people clearly see his face. I only remembered it a little earlier today. Though the young woman had claimed no injury, I wished to be sure of it." Kathryn appeared to be in control of her feelings. This was not going as planned.

"It was too late that night to awaken the household for a situation in which nothing could be done. I should have mentioned it the next day, but I remember thinking that I should more than likely see her during my stay. When I thought of it while dressing for dinner, I supposed it to be a neighbor I had not yet encountered and decided I should tell Sir John this evening. I have been remiss in my actions, and I am sorry."

"By Jove, ain't heard nothing about it, ain't heard a thing." Sir John was almost as agitated as his daughter. "What are we coming to when old Trotton becomes the playground of thieves and assassins? I'd best question the neighborhood, my boy, get to the bottom of all this, what?"

"I assure you, Sir John, I had no intention of raising such alarms. I truly believe the fellow long gone."

"Perhaps, my lord," Kathryn began, "if you could

describe the lady you saw, Sir John might go right to the source without alarming the entire neighborhood."

"A smart girl that, very smart indeed," muttered Sir John.

"I am afraid I can give very little description. She wore a hooded cloak, and as I mentioned, it was very late. I would guess she was young, based on her voice, and she was of a height approximately the same as Miss Charity."

Dalton had been a little taken aback by Kathryn's request. He soon realized, however, that she wanted Sir John and the rest to determine the woman was not one of the locals. Should that be the case, there need be no widespread search nor any investigation. She understood perfectly what he was doing, and she was doing everything in her power to stop it.

But Charity was having none of his indifference. "And what of her figure, my lord? Surely you did not let that escape your notice." Her eyes flashed fire, and jealousy dripped from her words.

Would no one in this house stand up to the girl?

"I do not suppose it would have, Miss Charity, but as I mentioned, the woman was wearing a cloak, leaving me no clear indication of it." He looked for a moment at his plate. "That is all I remember. I fear I have been of little help."

Charity finally seemed to accept Lord Dalton's air of nonchalance and was willing to allow a few more moments of discussion on the topic in order to add to her own consequence. "Papa, I should know if such a thing occurred amongst any of the women. We must suppose she was a stranger, too."

Kathryn's ploy appeared to be working.

"You would know of any of the gentry, my love," Lady Dinsmore chimed in, "but none of us could be sure of all the tenants and villagers. She could even be a servant for one of our local families. We must hope, since we have not heard of the unfortunate affair, that the woman truly was uninjured."

Suddenly Kathryn spoke up, and he felt the anger in her words. "I am in agreement, my lady." She turned to look him fully in the face, though he could not see her eyes. "I believe to discuss it further would only cause alarm. I do not think you should let this *story* distress you."

He had not expected it. She had not been cowed by his actions and she did not sit by and submit to his words and darts. She had been a full participant, and he had been the one to look a fool.

If all she told him had been true, she had been beaten down and trodden upon by every male in her life. Did he want to be a part of that? He knew now that he did not.

He put his napkin on the table beside his plate. He was about to excuse himself when the butler entered the room and brought a silver salver with a letter upon it to him. "A missive has just arrived for you, my lord."

"Thank you, Jarvis."

He noticed that Kathryn used the diversion to excuse herself from the dining room.

He opened the vellum envelope and scanned the short note from his mother.

"Lord Dalton, I do hope it is not bad news," exclaimed Lady Dinsmore.

"Not bad, precisely, but I must leave for Rye first thing in the morning."

Charity chimed in before her mother could stop her. "Leave tomorrow? Again? What about the party? The invitations have gone out! What will my friends think?"

"I am sorry, Miss Charity, Lady Dinsmore, but my steward informs me there is an urgent matter I need to address." He watched the two fallen faces before him and felt guilty about the expense they had gone to for the affair.

"I shall not spoil your plans, Lady Dinsmore." He purposely avoided the eyes of her daughter. "I need only spend one night away to handle a few matters. I shall return the day after tomorrow. I still have plans to find the last two horses I will need."

Charity clapped in delight like a schoolgirl. He had no doubt she thought his return had something to do with her. He moved his chair out of the way and rolled his eyes as he left the room.

As he started for the staircase, Kathryn appeared before him, shoulders squared and a fire in her bearing.

"My lord, I beg a word with you."

"Very well."

"I do not wish to make a *public* scene here in the hallway. Will you attend me in the small drawing room?"

He motioned for her to lead the way.

She went to the fireplace and took off her spectacles as she turned to face him. He was, in truth, astonished!

"I have little time, my lord, as you well know, but I have had enough. I want to look you in the eye and tell you if you *ever* do anything like that again, I vow I will give this up. I will go to Lady Dinsmore myself and tell her the truth, no matter what the cost to those children. What you just did had nothing to do with them.

"You needed to hurt me because of your anger, and I have allowed it. But this time you almost hurt them." He could see her shaking in her anger.

She balled her fists at her sides. "I deserve everything and more that you want to do to me." He tried to interrupt her, but she held up her hand to silence him. "This is as close to a family as I have right now, and I will not let you hurt them. In your effort to demean me, you instilled a fear in them that was a sham. Sir John could have sent word to all of the local families warning them to be on their guard. I will not have it. Do you understand?"

"Yes, yes, I do, Kathryn." He moved a little nearer. "I apologize. You are right. I had no business dragging them into our quarrel. I am sorry."

She stared into his eyes, and if looks could kill, he would be laid out on the beautiful Aubusson carpet. He tried to convey real remorse, but she stopped him again.

"Very well, my lord. I will take you at your word." With that, she put on her glasses and strode past him, slamming the door behind her.

Chapter Ten

The missive he received had been minor in nature, but he used it as an excuse to leave the manor, anyway. He wanted to see Kathryn's father.

She was adamant he would never forgive her, and he found himself needing to be reminded why he should not do the same. The cutting remarks had never been gratifying, and the anger he had experienced while in London had not been sustained by the torture he inflicted on her.

It was time he sought the full truth, and her father was the only other person who knew it.

Dalton arrived at Montgomery Hall as dusk fell over the countryside. His thoughts had all been of Kathryn. He was confused, angry and heartsore.

When she had berated him the evening before, he was sincere in his apologies. He was a gentleman, by Jove, and he had put the whole family in a taking just to get back at her. He thought he had sunk very low indeed.

He realized her father might actually be the only other person who would understand what he was going through. He, too, would have felt mortally wounded and changed forever by the route she had chosen to take.

The unwanted conviction reared its ugly head once again. Should an action taken at seventeen years of age by a very green girl be so harshly judged? It did not diminish his pain, but it made him second-guess his plan of retribution.

He had decided that he would not carry his hurt and anger into the meeting with her father, but an unexpected stop when one of his leaders threw a shoe, and a crowded inn that took almost an hour to get a change of horses, frustrated him beyond measure.

Therefore, when the butler tried to turn him away, stating that his master was not at home to callers, his promise flew out the window.

He handed the butler his card with the corner turned down, indicating he was present and waiting to see the marquis. "Do you plan to leave me on the doorstep like some tradesman, or may I come in and wait while you deliver my message to your master?" It was said with gritted teeth and a tic in his jaw, leaving the butler in no doubt as to his intent.

Donaldson had been employed at Montgomery Hall for more than thirty years. He was not cowed. "Lord Dalton, you may come in and you may wait while your card is given to His Lordship. However, the outcome will be the same." He was apparently allowed much freedom due to his tenure, but he had caught Lord Dalton on a bad day. "I will wait here until I see your master, so the sooner you get the message to him, the sooner you may go about your business."

What was wrong with him? His anger seemed to permeate his soul. He was never rude to servants, or of a demanding nature. Was he allowing the bitterness his mother talked to him about to seep into every area of his life now that Kathryn was back in it? *Lord, forgive my actions and my attitude. I have allowed circumstances to tempt me into rudeness. Please help me in the meeting with the marquis.*

He turned when he heard the door to the drawing room open, but it was neither Kathryn's father nor the butler.

"Lord Dalton." The man bowed low. "I am Hendrick, His Lordship's valet." He cleared his throat. "I shall take you to the master directly—however, I must inform you that he has been quite ill. We fear for his recovery, as he is not strong. The doctors have advised him against seeing visitors, but when he saw your card, he would not be gainsaid." He walked back to the door, indicating that Lord Dalton should precede him into the hallway.

"You must prepare yourself, my lord. He has been sick for some time and is not as…robust as you may remember him." As they began their ascent to the upper floors, the valet stopped and faced him. "He is very weak, my lord, and must not be upset. I tell you now that I will take it upon myself to remove you should I deem it necessary."

Dalton was completely taken aback. He had not known what to expect, but this had never occurred to him. "I understand, Hendrick, and I appreciate your dedication to your master."

He was ushered into a massive bedchamber with the curtains drawn and many candles already lit. He looked toward the bed and saw two male servants settling a frail man into a sitting position against a mountain of pillows. All harshness and anger left him, and he waited patiently for the marquis's attention. When the servants finally moved away, the man in the bed was out of breath and deathly pale. God's truth, he *was* a shell of the man he remembered.

"My boy, I am sorry…" he said, drawing a ragged breath. "Sorry for making you wait so long. I…do not get many…visitors these days."

"My lord, it is I who am sorry. I came here with an angry heart, and I bullied my way into disrupting your peace. I did not know you were unwell. I apologize, sir." He was sincerely sorry; it showed clearly on his face.

"Nonsense! My servants have been threatening you, have they?" He gave a weak smile. "They are so loyal," he said, still a little out of breath, "that they watch me like a hawk. I got to throw my weight around today. It feels good." He lay back against the pillows and closed his eyes, but with the smile still on his face.

Dalton did not know what to do. Had they not gotten him into a sitting position, he would have begged the man's pardon and retreated. But Kathryn's father had clearly been intent on seeing him, as well, despite his illness.

"Pull one of those chairs up close to me, son. Have no fear—I am not contagious."

"My lord," Dalton said as he brought a chair from the fireplace, "may I ask what your doctors *have* diagnosed?"

"I am fed up with the lot of them, if you want the truth with no bark on it. They say I had the influenza first and that it moved into my lungs. They tell me it has turned into pneumonia, and frankly, they are surprised I still live." He suddenly began to cough, and Hendrick ran for a glass of water while Dalton instinctively went to support his head as he drank.

"My lord, it is time for your next draft."

"No, no, go away. You may administer it when Lord Dalton has settled in for the night. I wish to have a clear head at the moment."

As the valet left the room, Dalton's heart hurt him. This visit was years too late, and this man was all alone except for his loyal servants. "My lord, perhaps…"

"Call me Edward, please. And there is no point in putting this off until I am better. I…" He fought for some air. "I wish to speak to you. I *need* to speak to you." He closed his eyes after calming his cough, but he opened them again and looked at him piercingly. "Tell me you have found her. Please tell me you know where she is."

"I beg your pardon? Can it be that you do not? I thought— I was under the impression you had no wish to know where she was."

He laid his head back, though he still watched him. His voice was low. "I do not know. She would be with me if I did."

Dalton ran his hands through his hair. He had come

here to share disappointment and empathy about Kathryn. He had come to ask him why he had not had the decency to let him know the truth about her so long ago. He had not told him because he had not known.

"Yes sir, I know where she is."

The man's eyes closed again, and Dalton saw his entire body relax. "Tell me everything."

"I am afraid that is what I wished of you."

"I do not understand. You have found her, you have spoken with her. Did she not tell you what happened? What a complete fool I was? Where has she been? Is she well? Would she… Do you think she could ever be convinced to see me again?"

"Sir, perhaps you had better rest while I speak. I fear there are parts that may be difficult for you if you have had no conversation with her since she eloped."

"I have had no communication with *her,* but when I discovered Salford was back in London, you may be sure I had a serious discussion with him." He leaned his head back again. "He said she refused to marry him. He said *she* used *him* to meet a…lover in Scotland. I did not believe it of her, ever! But I had men looking for her as soon as the next morning. None could trace her." The back of his thin, translucent hand came up to cover his eyes. "Lord Salford will not show his face in England again if he knows what is good for him."

"I have discovered he is now deceased, my lord."

"I am glad to hear it, though I will have to confess that to God. I was such a fool. I wrote her that she was no longer my daughter. And she believed me. I have lived with that for all these years, but I told God He could do with me what He would, as long as He kept her safe. I hope that is why I am sick, so she may be well."

"I will tell you the circumstances under which we met, and what she has told me of her life. I came to you angry, wanting to know the reason you had not told me why she left London with no one the wiser. I can see now that all three of us have been at cross purposes."

Dalton was worried about the man so ill before him. Should he tell him everything? Should he keep some things between Kathryn and himself? He decided he would tell him all of it, since he would want nothing less if it were him. But he would lessen the extremity of some things.

As he finished his tale with the recounting of their meeting, he would have suspected the man had drifted off to sleep except for the tears rolling out of his closed eyes.

Dalton confessed, "I was rude and appalled and hurt to the core of my heart. But I still could not let it rest. Or perhaps God would not let me leave it that way. Now that He has forgiven me my anger, I believe it is I who was the fool." He gave a bitter laugh as he quoted the verse his mother told him to lean on in this situation: *"And be ye kind one to another, tenderhearted, forgiving one another..."*

"You still love her, too." The older man believed it; he did not ask it.

The answer was not so clear to him. "I do not know, sir. We have been apart a long time, and we have both matured a great deal. Does that new maturity lend itself to an old love? I am afraid I have not given it even half a chance."

The two sat in silence for a moment. Her father saw all the things he loved about her, but he had been too angry to trust his feelings. Was it too late to make up for the lost nine years?

"Will you bring her to see me?"

The person he had loved so long ago was not the same person now. Indeed, *he* was not the same person now. But he knew fundamentally, she had not changed. She was more mature, yes, but she was also more nurturing, more protective, and willing to fight for those she loved. It was all new to him.

He asked again, "Will you bring her to see me?"

"I will need to be sure she will believe *me* first, but then I will bring her. It may take me a little time, but if it is within my power, I will bring her."

"Thank you, my boy, but time is the one thing I may not have."

Dalton determined he would expedite a reunion between Kathryn and her father if he had to tie her up to do it. In the meantime, there was much he had to do.

That night, in a guest chamber of Montgomery Hall, Dalton lay awake a long time into the night. He thought back to the meeting between him and Kathryn's father when he had asked for her hand. He remembered it as if it were yesterday.

"Have a seat, son, welcome." The Marquis sat behind the desk. They were in the library in the house in Town.

Dalton was nervous. He had little to recommend him as the younger son of an earl.

"Sir, I have come to ask you...to get your permission..."

"To marry my daughter?"

"Yes, sir."

Her father got up and came around his desk to sit in the chair next to his. "My boy, there is no need to keep you on pins and needles. I know your parents, and I know you follow God in all things. Kathryn has mentioned to me that you talk of entering the War Office as a profession. I see no impediments, and I am thankful God has brought such a man into her life."

"Thank you, sir. That is high praise indeed, coming from a man I respect as much as you."

"Before we call on the lawyers to make the marriage settlements, I still have one question."

"You do not need to say it, sir. I know she is very young."

"That is it, my boy. She has had to grow up quicker than most because of the death of her mother. But her experience with men is only what she has gained in the last two months. I believe she loves you. I have no fear on that score."

"My lord, I have talked this over with my parents, and we all share the same concern. May I propose that we say nothing to Lady Kathryn at this time? Perhaps, if she still feels the same about me at the end of the Season, I will ask her to marry me?"

"Are you willing to risk that, my boy? I would never ask it of you."

"As I said, I have thought this through. I hope that your approval will allow me as much time with her as I need for her to get to know me fully. If she finds someone she prefers over me, I should like to know it sooner rather than later."

"You have a good head on your shoulders, son. I agree with you that we should proceed in this way."

"And I have your permission to ask her when the time is right?"

No. He was as culpable in her running away as she was. Had he asked her to marry him as soon as her father had granted his permission, the elopement may never have occurred.

Dear God, how will I ever confess this to her? How will I ever make it up to her?

Would she even let him make it up to her? Kathryn's father had asked him if he still loved her, and he'd answered truthfully: he did not know. But that wasn't the entire truth. He knew he did not *still* love her. But as each day passed together at Dinsmore Manor, and each moment a new revelation came to light, it made him think that perhaps he could love her *again*.

She was different, more mature, but so was he. He realized, as he regaled her father with each of her characteristics and the bravery with which she had faced each obstacle, that he was the one whose heart was being touched.

He would do everything in his power now to reunite Kathryn and her father. His time might be short, so that would be paramount. But after…he would begin to follow his heart again instead of his ego and pride.

Maybe that is what he should have done from the beginning.

Chapter Eleven

Lord Dalton no sooner returned midday from his trip than Master Jacob began triumphantly spreading the news that he had promised to spend the afternoon with them for the express purpose of building a moat. It appeared to Kathryn that Lord Dalton was surprised to hear it, but he never gave the child one cause to doubt him.

He bowed in earnest, greeting each occupant with a smile. "Miss Montgomery, I hope you are going to join us." Kathryn became wary, but he bowed and she gave the required curtsy.

"Lord Darling, you must stop smiling at Miss Montgomery and help me."

"You will wish I was smiling once you discover what a taskmaster I am," Dalton said, though ruffling the boy's hair belied his words. "But we will go softer on the ladies, I think, Master Jacob. What say you?"

"Oh, no, my lord. Lacey and I have our own plans for the morning. Have no fear." Kathryn hoped he did not see Lacey's face fall, or he would know how much the little girl wanted to be included.

"Not so fast, ma'am. Jacob and I will need underlings to do our bidding. We could not possibly dirty our hands with the project!"

Kathryn did not understand the change in him, and did not relish the idea of such close proximity to him for the entire morning. But he insisted it was a group project; she *must* stay.

She feared there was more to this visit than a simple promise to an eight-year-old, but as a relative servant, she could not gainsay an earl. She accepted, therefore, with more grace than she felt. Much of the night she had lain awake, thinking about the severe set down she had given him the night before. She believed her disguise hurt no one in the Dinsmore family. Lord Dalton's awareness of the lie perpetrated on them changed everything.

Lacey was delighted to be included and clapped with glee, making Lord Dalton laugh. Kathryn admitted defeat. It appeared Lacey did not feel the same about the fun they would have had on their own, after all. In short shrift, all four sat cross-legged on the floor around the tower. The children's nurse, knitting in the rocker by the window, chuckled several times to herself.

After deciding on the basic materials they would need for construction, Jacob raised the question that seemed to be pressing most on his mind. "But sir, how will we keep the water from leaking out? Nurse would scold us if we made such a mess on the floor."

Kathryn hated to be the bearer of bad news, but she

reminded him of his promise. "Jacob, I am sorry, but you may not use real water at all. You agreed to that the day we decided to build it."

"Jacob," Lord Dalton chimed in, "a man always keeps his word. So, I have been pondering the problem and I believe I have finally hit upon a solution that will satisfy all of our needs."

Kathryn and the children watched as Lord Dalton reached into his inner coat pocket and very slowly pull out a strip of dark blue shimmering fabric, much the way a magician would pull a handkerchief from his sleeve.

While the children looked at him in question, Kathryn knew exactly what she was looking at. She was, however, as puzzled as the children as to the material's purpose. "Lord Dalton, why have you taken a piece of the fabric that is hanging in the ballroom?"

"Ah, I see I shall have to watch my step. It seems we have a detective *disguised* as a companion in the house!"

Kathryn blushed to the roots of her hair, and she thought she saw regret in his face as he looked at her.

"I do not understand, either, sir," said Lacey, interrupting her thoughts.

"I have no real conviction it will work. I hope we can make our moat *appear* as if it were water."

The children were still a little uncertain, and Jacob was obviously disappointed at the pretense, but Kathryn joined in, determined that the children's day would not be ruined by their contretemps. "I see!" she exclaimed, and leaned across Lacey's lap with her hand outstretched, silently asking Lord Dalton for the material. Then she looked around for Lacey's drawing pad.

Upon finding it, she pulled several pieces of the large paper free and began to bunch them into paper balls of various shapes and sizes. Then she gently draped the blue shimmering fabric loosely over them. The chorus of "ahhs" that arose told her they had caught on, and Jacob and Lacey even went so far as to call Lord Dalton a wonderful moat maker.

All materials and plans now accounted for, the children began working in earnest while Kathryn and Lord Dalton offered a helping hand now and again. "Kath… Miss Montgomery, I *am* impressed! However did you arrive at such a brilliant idea so quickly?"

She made light of it with him, then excused herself for a moment to go back into the nursery. She was startled to find him behind her when she turned. "My lord?"

"I beg your pardon. I have noticed in my short stay here how well those two work together. I thought they would be fine on their own for a while, and then they could honestly proclaim their hard work when it is finished."

Kathryn saw a glimpse of the kindness he showed others bestowed upon her, and she felt confusion. His kindness always made her proud, though she knew it from many years ago. "I only came to retrieve one of the school chairs," she said as she put one hand around the newel post. "I was growing uncomfortable on the floor."

Lord Dalton gently lifted the chair from her hand

and grabbed another for himself. She retreated into the book room and he followed, making her feel uneasy. He set the chairs beside each other, close to where the children worked.

He stood behind her chair, as if holding it for her, so there was little she could do in rearranging them. He sat next to her but turned his attention back to the children. What was this new game? Did he think to gain her friendship again, only waiting for a better opportunity to humiliate her? "I should like to know, my lord, which part of the large dining room your material was taken from." She started to rise. "I suppose I had better remove there posthaste before Charity or her mother catch a glimpse of the damage."

"Come, Kath…Miss Montgomery, I vow you know me better than that! I cut the piece from the extra material hanging behind the draperies. No one will notice anything wrong, I assure you."

He ran his hand through his hair, and Kathryn knew that meant he was frustrated. " I apologize for treating you with such disrespect. I had no right, and I am truly sorry for it. If you wish me to somehow make reparation to the Dinsmore family, only say the word."

Kathryn was caught off guard again. "My lord," she said very quietly, "you have treated me as I deserve. The only apology I sought was on behalf of them."

"No." He seemed tongue-tied.

"You are only here for a few more days, and you may be as mean to *me* as you wish, if it lessens the torment I put you through."

He shook his head, unable to express himself fully

in front of the children. "I should like to impose upon you if you will consent to it."

With eyebrows furrowed, Kathryn just stared at him. She heard despair in his voice and could only wonder at it.

"May I ask when your next day off might be?"

"I do not understand, my lord."

"I know as an employee here, you may not be able to come and go as you please. I would like...I wished to take you...great guns! If you will spare the time to me on your next day off, I would appreciate it."

"Lord Dalton, my *half* day off is the day after the party. But I do not see how..."

"I know you do not, but I cannot discuss it in front of the children. Is it possible to take a full day? I am sorry. I obviously have much to learn about those who work in a household. Those who work in *my* household!"

Kathryn knew she was not the best judge, but he seemed sincere. However, she would not risk her heart again so soon. "I believe Lady Dinsmore would allow it if I asked, but as I have never done so before, I fear she will be interested to know why."

They were interrupted by Jacob, who grabbed Lord Dalton's hand and begged him to come see what they had done. "It *does* look like water, sir!"

After a quick "Excuse me, my lord." She rose and went out to the nurse, still knitting in her rocking chair. "Sally, will you keep an eye on these three for a few moments? I must check on the...ice sculpture for the party." She was halfway out the door before Lord Dalton could stop her.

Sally chuckled and waved her on. "It ain't the two wee ones I'll be having to restrain, miss," she said to no one in particular, as Miss Montgomery was gone and Lord Dalton not far behind.

Kathryn ran down the hallway as soon as she left the nursery and went straight to the large dining room where the party would be held. She decided, if found, she had any number of reasons for being there. She stood at the French doors, surrounded by what she would always think of as Vauxhall Gardens, and tried to calm her fluttering heart.

Lord Dalton's voice behind her had the opposite effect. "Kathryn, what is it?" He put his hands on her shoulders and gently turned her toward him.

"My lord, there is no need to manhandle me."

He let her go so quickly she almost tumbled backward. "I beg your pardon," he said.

She did not know what to think. She was so confused. He was being quite civil today, which was more than she could say about his behavior two nights ago, or any of the time since he had returned, for that matter.

"What is it you want from me, my lord?"

"I want you to trust me in this."

She turned her back on him and looked out the glass doors once again.

"I know I have behaved despicably. And I know I have given you no reason to trust me since I found out…discovered…it was you. But I would like to take you with me to visit someone we both need to see. We will not be able to do that in half a day."

She turned back to him. "Who would we be visiting?" she asked curtly.

"I decided I would ask you to trust me and believe it is someone you wish to see, but I fear I have not earned that trust yet, so I will tell you."

She saw that it was he who was uncomfortable now, but was not in the mood to humor him.

"It is your father."

She gasped and came at him with fists balled in rage. "How *dare* you?"

He grabbed her fists before she could do damage he had no doubt she could do. "He wants to see you, Kathryn. He needs to see you. And I think, from all you have said, you need to see him, too."

"You have no idea what I need. And why would you have seen my father? Is this another means of punishing me, my lord? I own it is your best effort to date."

She tried to pull away. What was he doing? If he was so set on defeating her, why did he not just leave? She was stuck in a lifetime of servitude. Was that not enough for him?

"Kathryn, hear me, please. When you told me your story, I could not fathom that no one had seen you in all these years." He still held her hands. "I confess I was as angry at him as I was at you. I felt I deserved to know why he had not told me about the elopement. It was as if I had never been a part of either of your lives.

"So I went to see him. He is sorry, Kathryn. I know I have no right to ask it of you, and you could certainly go see him quite on your own. But I believe if we both go, it will do each of us good. Maybe help us understand each other and what has happened between then and now. I *know* it would be the best thing for him."

"Is this the same speech you gave him, my lord?"

"No! I went to see him for my own selfish reasons. He asked me to bring you to him, if you would come."

"*He* asked for *me?*" Her surprise was real, but became jaded in an instant. "Why should I believe you?"

"I think he should be the one to tell you his reasoning, not I." He pulled both of her hands up to his chest, knowing the pain and anger that would be in her eyes, though he could not see them. "I have been unkind and cruel to you. I wish I had not, but I cannot undo it. I wish the hard feelings to end here. I have sought God's forgiveness, and I ask now for yours. I know you will need time. But please say you will go with me to see him on your day off. No one will know you are with me, I promise."

"I…"

She spoke but the one word before Charity and her mother entered the room and were brought up short at the sight of Lord Dalton holding her hands.

"Miss Montgomery!" screeched Charity at her vilest.

"Miss Montgomery!" said Lady Dinsmore at the same time, and in complete shock. "What am I to understand by this…this…display?"

Drat the man! Kathryn had allowed time alone with him to cloud her judgment, and she was no doubt about to lose her position because of it. She quickly pulled her hands from Lord Dalton's and rested them at her side. "Lady Dinsmore," she began, but was cut off mid-breath by the man standing beside her.

"Lady Dinsmore, to what do you refer?" asked Lord Dalton, who sounded completely bewildered. "Oh, I see. You are referring to my holding Miss Montgomery's hands? Your expression quite shocked me a moment ago."

"Do not dissemble, *my lord*." Charity's tone was dripping with disgust. "You have been dallying with our servant. You, sir, are no gentleman! The situation must be rectified."

The smile was immediately erased from Lord Dalton's face, and Lady Dinsmore elbowed her irksome daughter, whispering, "Charity, be still. You go too far."

The tone of steel in Lord Dalton's voice decided Charity's reticence as her mother's hasty warning had not. "No one in this house has been dallied with by me, and I resent your accusation even more on the part of Miss Montgomery. You owe her an abject apology on the instant."

Lady Dinsmore tried to assuage Lord Dalton's temper before Charity made any more stupid remarks. "My lord, you must not take Charity's words to heart. She reads too many novels, and I believe they are quite unfit for such young minds." She chuckled and came a little closer. "It gives them such a flair for the dramatic. It makes you want to quite laugh at them."

"I assure you, madam," he said in an icy voice, "I am not laughing."

"But Mama, he was holding her hands—you saw it as well as I," cried the confused young beauty.

"Lady Dinsmore," said the earl, "I can see that an explanation is due *you*." He emphasized the elder woman with a look of disdain for the younger. "But an apology is also necessary for the aspersions cast on a very honorable woman, whether an explanation were forthcoming or not."

"Please," cried Kathryn, "an apology is *not* necessary. I am aware this situation appears questionable...." She stopped, realizing that Lord Dalton's explanation was certainly not clear to her; therefore, she could not offer it. "Can we not forget the entire matter?" She lowered her voice, wishing the floor would open up and swallow her. "May I please return to my room?"

"Lady Dinsmore," said the highly indignant earl, "I know it is not a common thought that women have a code of honor."

Kathryn's eyes widened, and her mouth fell open at the audacity of the man before her.

"But I believe," he continued, "women can be just as honorable as men, and if your daughter and Miss Montgomery *were* men, no less than the satisfaction of a duel would accompany those words."

Kathryn felt joy for the first time in a long time, and she wanted to give him a standing ovation with thunderous applause. But sadness crept in as she imagined the enjoyment they might have had for a lifetime had she not made her mistake.

The word *duel* had the desired effect, and Charity blanched before quickly offering a shaky apology to her wayward companion. As if Lord Dalton had ever fought in a duel!

Between clenched teeth and with disjointed sentences, the beauty ground out her apology. "I beg your pardon, Miss Montgomery. I thought…I thought you might be in need of our assistance. I see I have totally misconstrued the situation. I never intended to question your honor. Forgive me for any slight you may have taken." Her fists balled at her side added to the appearance that the apology was torn from her lips.

Charity looked at Lord Dalton for approval, which was all to the good. Had she waited for a response from Kathryn, she would have waited a long time.

He made the pretense of visibly relaxing, to let the encroaching chit know an actual duel had been averted. Though he did not know it, Kathryn could not wait to hear his next words.

"Very pretty, Miss Charity," he generously offered. "I am sure Miss Montgomery has taken no offense." He looked at Kathryn with raised eyebrows, expecting her assent.

She nodded stoically, now terribly afraid if she had to speak one word, a fit of laughter would overtake her.

"Lady Dinsmore," he continued, "that explanation I promised you…"

"Oh, it is quite unnecessary, my lord," said the toadying woman. "Miss Montgomery always behaves above reproach—you have no need to defend her to me."

"Defend her?" He seemed dumbfounded. "No, indeed, I should think not. I owe you an explanation about your decorations."

All three women now looked at the man before them, and he continued as if nothing out of the ordinary was taking place. "You see, I was afraid Master

Jacob would want to use real water in the moat of his Martello Tower."

"Moat? I…I…see," muttered the lady, with no inkling whatsoever as to what he was talking about.

"Hence," the earl continued, "I devised what I thought to be a perfect plan and snipped some of this shimmery blue material to take to the nursery with me. It would make the moat appear to *look* like water."

"Martello Tower…" the befuddled woman echoed.

"The children were delighted with it, but Miss Montgomery gave me the scolding of my life." He leaned closer to whisper to Lady Dinsmore, aware that they could hear every word he was saying. "She can be a bit of a termagant when angry, can she not?" Standing tall again, he said, "She demanded at once that I show her where I had cut the fabric, worried that all of your hard work might be damaged. I showed her that I took a piece from behind the draperies so as not to be noticeable. However, when she wished to assure herself of the truth of my words, one of the pins holding the fabric in place pricked her finger."

"Cut a piece…?" said Lady Dinsmore, no longer even pretending to understand.

"I was examining her injury when you entered the room. I apologize again for any concern I might have given by using your party decorations."

"To be sure…of course…as I said, no need for apologies."

"Capital! Now if you will excuse us, we must return to the nursery to help Master Jacob finish the moat." He turned and held a hand toward the door, indicating Miss Montgomery should precede him, which she did. "We shall join you again at tea. Good day, ladies."

Kathryn heard the door to the dining room close behind them, but hurried toward the stairs, unable to keep a straight face, and afraid she would burst out laughing while still within earshot of her employer. "Of all the horrible performances I have seen in my life…"

"Tell me quickly, Kathryn, before we are interrupted again. Will you go with me to see your father?"

"I will think on it, my lord." She did not tell him it terrified her to her very core. She did not think she could bear one more act of vengeance for the pain she had wrought so many years before.

Chapter Twelve

With the contretemps earlier in the decorated dining hall, Kathryn was certain Mrs. Wimpole would suddenly be available to accompany her husband to dinner that night. So it came as quite a shock to hear a knock on the housekeeper's door as a footman politely reminded her that the house awaited her arrival in the drawing room. She thanked him and then hastily ran to her room to wash her face and tidy her hair. That she had already eaten with the servants never crossed her mind.

She knew Lady Dinsmore must have considered it, but in the end, the lady would have reasoned Lord Dalton might take offense at her absence. A harried Kathryn entered the drawing room, and all eyes turned to her. She could only assume they had been speaking of her, so she curtsied and said at once, "I beg your pardon. I did not hear the dinner bell. Please forgive me for keeping you waiting."

Kathryn took a quick glance at Lord Dalton. She

knew no one would notice her looking from behind her glasses. But she saw all she needed to know in *his* eyes. He was angry, and he started toward her. Fortunately, he was halted by Charity's voice.

"Pay it no mind, Kate," said Charity, fawning as she herself came to the side of her companion. "We are only just ready to go in, and you have appeared in plenty of time. Here," she said cordially, linking arms with a dumbfounded Kathryn, "what do you say *we* lead the dinner procession this evening? We shall cut a new dash!"

Charity must have been taken severely to task and was now dumping the butter boat over her. It appeared as if the young beauty finally understood Kathryn's discourses on her temper, and began using the power of flattery in her quest to win the earl.

At dinner, it seemed to Kathryn that Lord Dalton accepted Charity's attention happily. She could not stop herself from glancing across the table at him, and she thought he met her gaze on more than one occasion. He had been so different this afternoon—almost kind, but he now appeared to be perfectly content. And if it irritated her, then all the better.

After dinner, the ladies left the men to go into the drawing room, Lady Dinsmore taking Kathryn's arm. "I wished to leave while we were on such pleasant footing. I am hoping charitable feelings will carry us through the rest of the evening."

Kathryn had tried to excuse herself from the drawing room, but Lady Dinsmore was having none of it. "What with all of the work you have done for the party, you deserve a pleasant evening enjoying yourself." Kathryn was surprised. With Charity on her best behavior, now would be the time to allow her to be alone with Lord Dalton, fully supervised by her parents and the vicar, but without her companion sharing his attention.

Lady Dinsmore stopped and turned to face her. "Kate, you have forgiven us the gaffe from this afternoon, have you not? I would not have had it happen for the world."

"Please, my lady, you must have no fear on that score. It is I who am to blame. If we could all forget it ever happened, I would be quite content." She certainly did not wish to be a fly in the ointment on this, their most affable evening to date. "If Charity agrees, I will join you."

"Delightful! You may have guessed I gave her quite a dressing-down." Kathryn closed her eyes for one second and sighed. Charity would only take so much from her mother before she would once again show complete disdain for her companion.

"I wish you had not, my lady."

"Have no fear—it is now all forgotten."

Lady Dinsmore may have forgotten it, but Kathryn had not. She had very little time to process Lord Dalton's about-face and the discovery that he went to see her father. She did not know if she would go to see him. She wanted to, but nine years of abandonment could not be fixed in a day. Indeed, it might never be fixed.

As the gentlemen returned from the dining room, all Kathryn could think of was getting to her room. She suspected her reflections on this day would certainly keep her awake until the wee hours of the morning.

While sitting with Sir John and the vicar, Dalton lost track of the discussion of local people and places of which he had no knowledge. His thoughts drifted back over his own day, and he found himself smiling. The time with the children had saved him from Charity's grasp, but more than that, he thought he had taken a small step in the battle to end the confrontation between him and Kathryn. And suddenly he wanted the war to end. Would she let it?

When they were alone those few moments in the dining hall, he had been faced with a woman who had come down in the world, but had more dignity than any woman of his acquaintance. He did not suppose he could think much higher of the intelligent, thoughtful woman he had loved nine years ago, but he saw a maturity that could only have been attained through the horrors of her life, horrors she did not succumb to. His estimation *had* risen, and he prayed that even if she could not bear him, she would at least see her father.

As far as he was concerned, it would take quite a bit more. And he was beginning to believe he had wasted the past two weeks. It was time that could have been spent getting to know her better, as she was now.

All of the qualities he was discovering in the gentle woman were beginning to change his view on women as a whole. He knew she had a wonderful sense of humor, but as he acted out the farce in the party room that afternoon, he was delighted that she had been so in tune with him, though she tried to hide it.

It was not just beauty or intelligence, or even a sense of humor. It included the full gamut of characteristics. He was in the presence of an honorable woman, despite the things that had happened in her life and the lengths she had gone to that had brought her to this place.

His musings were interrupted by Sir John. "Shall we join the ladies, my lord? Quite sure we should, before they come looking for us!" He laughed at his own joke, and the three of them repaired to the drawing room.

Upon entering, he could hear Charity once again abusing Kathryn for some slight. The recalcitrant child had not even made it through one evening with the polite behavior she showed before and during dinner.

Dalton was no fool. Kathryn was late for dinner because she had fully expected to be excluded from it. He had believed it himself until she appeared, a bit disheveled, in the drawing room. He began to take himself to task and wonder if any of his own people were treated with so little feeling. Had he himself been guilty of it?

"Oh, my lord," Charity simpered, intruding on his thoughts. "Shall we play cards this evening? I am sure Mr. Wimpole and Kate will be happy to make up a foursome." She gave no thought to the two she felt were completely beneath her.

He would begin to scrutinize the depths of the contenders for his heart much more closely from now on. The idea struck him—what if those contenders did not have the qualities and characteristics he saw in

Kathryn? He was quite sure he could not do without them now.

To say that it was the most frustrating game of cards he had ever been a part of would be an understatement. Charity, in actuality, had no interest in the game, only in being his partner so she could send the most ridiculous hints that were both completely against the rules and always veiled with two possible meanings. The vicar and Kathryn beat them soundly.

The tea tray was a blessing, and he purposely seated himself in a straight-backed chair where Charity could not join him. He was overjoyed when she volunteered to play the pianoforte for him. When she was safely seated and actually playing, he rose to get two cups of tea and moved to the settee where Kathryn sat. As he handed her a cup, one look at her face told him she was well aware of the reasoning for his actions.

"I begin to believe you have no control over your charge at all," he accused jovially.

"Too true," was all she mumbled.

"Indeed, it seems to me you are quite derelict in your duty."

Kathryn had moved to the pianoforte as Charity left it, and Lord Dalton once again joined her, this time with a plate of scones. "I cannot keep following you about the room. Your employers will think me after the post of your personal lackey. Now tell me how I am supposed to deal with the chit."

"My lord, you have only a few days left. I am unable to help you. She is my employer, if you will remember." And when he thought that was all she would say, she added, "You will make your escape quite soon."

She then stopped and pretended to ponder something. "You probably ought to prepare yourself for when she arrives in London. Your name will be the first member of the *ton* they associate themselves with, and everyone will think you have fallen head over heels for a beautiful nobody."

The plate of scones rolling across the floor let Kathryn know she had hit the mark. As he bent, embarrassed, to retrieve the flaky treats, she sauntered away, saying under her breath, "I do not think they would hire you as my lackey, sir. You are quite inept!"

Over the next two days, Kathryn was busy with the party preparations. She went over the menu with Cook, arranged all of the cut flowers throughout the house, made a seating chart now that all of the guests had accepted and oversaw the servants—all around the schedule of Charity and her needs. Indeed, she was so busy that the children finally tracked her down and asked if they could go on a picnic.

They were so ignored during the hustle and bustle that her heart hurt at their pleading faces. "My darlings, I believe that is exactly what we need! How smart you are." She told them they would have to get Nurse's approval, and they would have to be happy with whatever Cook could spare from the party preparations.

All was arranged, and they walked down to the lake and set their blanket under the beautiful weeping willow. Jacob had brought fishing poles, and the two children ran off with strict instructions that neither of them would get wet.

Kathryn thought this would be a perfect time to relax, but she found her thoughts turning to Lord Dalton and how she had made such a bumblebroth of everything.

How she wished things were different. She wished she could meet with him as herself. Perhaps if she agreed to see her father, she could be free of her disguise for a time.

"Miss Montgomery," the children cried, "look what we have caught!" Kathryn stared at the tiny fish still on Jacob's hook. She knew they must throw it back into the lake, but she hated to see the proud smile leave the little boy's face.

Sighing, she said, "He is very little. You must throw him back until he has time to grow up with the other fish."

The groans displayed their disappointment, but she knew they would obey her—not without a fight, however. "May we keep him in the bucket awhile and watch him swim? His fins help him swim very fast."

"Only for a little while, Jacob. He will grow tired of flapping his fins in that very small bucket." They ran back to the lake.

The thought of her father kept running through her mind.

What was she to do? Lord Dalton said her father had asked to see her. But what if that was only a hoax to get her there? He seemed less angry lately, but suppose it was all a ruse so he and her father would be able to drag her through the muddy past once again?

She should be paying closer attention to the children, but she could not erase her father from her mind completely.

No matter what she feared, could she overcome it long enough to see him again? It had been just the two of them since her mother died, up to the time she made her *mistake.* That was the beginning of their horrible estrangement. Even were he still as angry, she felt an aching need to see him again; whether the discord remained or not.

She would go with Lord Dalton, no matter what the outcome.

As she started to rise, his voice at her side startled her. "May I help you up, Kathryn?" He held her hand until she was steady. "You could have taken a nasty fall. Are you sure those shoes are absolutely necessary?"

She shook a little. "Thank you, my lord. And yes, I think they are." She could no longer tell whether his words were kind or more meant to hurt her.

The children came up to them, water sloshing out of both sides of the bucket. "Lord Darning, look at our fish, look at our fish."

"Lord *Dalton,* Jacob," Kathryn corrected him for the one-hundredth time.

"Whoa there, Master Jacob, did he put up much of a fight?"

Kathryn realized he would make a great father someday.

"No, he is just a baby fish. Miss Montgomery says

we must put him back, but we wanted to watch him for a while."

"She is quite right. And since she has such a difficult time staying on schedule, I have come to get you. I suspect you had better let him go now so we can get you properly cleaned up before appearing in the drawing room for tea."

"Oh, dear, I do not know what has come over me," Kathryn said. "But dawdling, when Lady Dinsmore puts so much stock in being on time, will not keep me employed overlong. Jacob, hurry down and release your fish. Lacey, can you gather the poles while he does that? I will put away the picnic things."

The children ran back to the water and Lord Dalton knelt beside Kathryn, helping her load the empty basket. They did not speak, but she was aware of his gaze upon her several times.

When the children returned, they walked to the house as one group until Lacey and Jacob ran ahead to put the fishing gear back into place.

"Kathryn?" Lord Dalton hesitated.

"Yes, my lord?"

"Please forgive my impatience *and* my impertinence, but I have not had a moment to speak with… To ask…" Kathryn took pity on him as he stumbled around the question.

"Yes, Lord Dalton, I will go to my father's house with you."

"God bless you, Kathryn!" He took hold of her swinging hand and kissed it. "I do not think you will be sorry."

His hasty action surprised her, and she found herself at a loss. Kathryn turned to him at last while easing her hand from his. "I have asked Lady Dinsmore if I may have the whole day to visit a distant relative. I did not need to add another lie to my long list of sins." She blushed and hurriedly went on. "You are supposed to take your leave that day. Am I to meet you somewhere?"

"I have asked Sir John if I may remain an extra day, as I have been called away again and am not completely decided on one horse."

She looked at him, and his slow smile produced two deep dimples.

The day before the party had been especially hectic, and Charity seemed to be especially needy.

"Kate, where have you put my white gloves?"

"Kate, you are certain Lord Dalton is seated at my side and that the Farnham twins are across from me?"

"Kate…"

"Kate…"

With final arrangements to check on, Charity's whining, and her presence required in the drawing room after dinner, Kathryn thought she might fall asleep while reading the children a story.

Lord Dalton kept busy with Sir John and his irksome daughter. Kathryn was well aware he deflected several of Charity's barbs and even went out of his way to keep her occupied. It only fueled the girl's belief that she had won him and that an announcement might still be made at the party. Kathryn seemed to be the only one who believed he would leave with nothing but horses.

There had been one part of this day particularly up-setting for Kathryn. Lady Dinsmore required her attendance tomorrow evening during the party.

"Please, my lady, I do not wish to be there. I told you when you hired me that going into Society makes me quite uncomfortable. I did as you asked and joined you for dinner each evening. Was that not enough?"

"Dear Kate, I realize the extra effort you have put forth since Lord Dalton has been with us. And I appreciate it, I certainly do. But with Charity the center of attention, which you know she will be despite the party being in honor of the earl, we shall have to be ready to avoid any unpleasant scenes."

For the first time, Kathryn felt the impulse to tell the woman before her that Charity's behavior had been unchecked for so long that it was not *her* responsibility to control it now. But in truth, that was in part why she had been hired, and she could not answer as she wished.

"But there is a second reason, my dear. You deserve your share of pleasure for once, especially after all the effort you have put forth. I wish you to enjoy yourself."

Kathryn did not explain that her idea of pleasure after all the work was to settle into bed with a good book until the next morning. But she did protest. "My lady, you must know by now that I find no pleasure in such entertainments. Indeed, you will be wondered at by your neighbors when they see Charity's companion in attendance."

"You give yourself too little credit. And you know perfectly well that all of our guests are already acquainted with you and have sung your praises since you came to us."

"But I have no gown. I shall stick out like a sore thumb."

"No such thing. Your blue muslin, the one you have been wearing to dinner, is lovely. You must not worry on that score. Now, I do not wish to hear another word. You are a valuable member of this household, and I desire your attendance."

It was only the thought that she was going to see her father again that allowed her to keep her composure. Two more days, and things would go back to normal—with a few brief memories of Lord Dalton tucked away for the future.

Chapter Thirteen

She was correct when she assumed she would be heavily pressed into service the entire day of the party. Therefore, when the florist delivered morning glories to a room decorated for an enchanted starry night, it was Kathryn who was required to deal with the incorrect order and Kathryn who was required to set it to rights.

The menu had to be checked and rechecked while Lady Dinsmore rested in the afternoon. The housekeeper must be pacified regularly if the house was expected to shine as brightly as the moonlit night sky of the large dining room.

Finally, evening arrived. An exhausted Kathryn was going up the stairs to change before returning for the party. On the way up, she passed the family descending. Their finery caused her a small pang of envy as her memory took her back to her own shining moment ages ago in London. Yet once she noticed Lord Dalton behind the ladies, all pining disappeared and she had thoughts only for him.

Was her sense that his rancor was fading true? Why would he bother to heal the rift between her and her father if he still held anger in his heart? He had kissed her hand! Was it a natural reaction based on his kindness, the kindness he had for all?

He looked exactly as she remembered at the balls a lifetime ago—completely in black but for his crisp white shirtfront and a silk waistcoat. His cravat was tied in the most intricate of folds, and it was even kept in place by the same sapphire stickpin she remembered. He once told her he began to wear it because it reminded him of her eyes.

"You all look quite splendid!" she said, afraid her notice of Lord Dalton was obvious to them.

He looked at her with a question in his eyes. "Are you not to join us?" She could not gauge the emotion behind the question, and how very embarrassed she was in her horrid disguise. But she put on a splendid front.

"I will return. I must change, and I promised I would let Jacob and Lacey watch for a short while." She curtsied prettily, and the group parted in the middle to allow her to pass through them.

Later, as she descended the same stairs, how she wished she had been adamant about not attending this party. She felt alone, completely alone. This one would be so different from the ones in her youthful days in London. She had been surrounded by friends *and* Lord Dalton. But she was only reminded that she had thrown that away.

Would forgiveness ever come? From anyone?

Well, she was Lady Kathryn. She had come down

in the world; she had lost her family and her home and was even forced into disguises to protect her safety. Her pride was long gone, but her intelligence and wits remained intact, and she would use them whether anyone noticed or not. She entered the dining hall, noticing how the candlelight and shimmering fabric made the room sparkle.

Servants passed her to and fro, nodding and smiling at one of their own. Kathryn sat against the wall, listening to the music and seeing the dancers drift by at a distance. She noticed Charity with Derek Farnham and realized that despite the girl's alarming temper, she would be the belle of her Season and be married within a month. She did not see Lord Dalton, and she realized she did not wish to see him twirling some local beauty around the dance floor. When had *her* anger abated?

"Kathryn," he said in a low voice, "will you grant me the next dance?"

Her eyes rose to meet his in surprise. He had appeared out of nowhere!

"Lord Dalton, what are you about?" she whispered. "You must dance with one of the women who were invited here for that exact purpose." She was embarrassed.

"I am greatly in need of rational conversation." He actually smiled at her. And when he did, the candlelight reflected the shimmering fabric and she thought there were real stars above. Just like Vauxhall Gardens nine years ago. "Do say you will rescue me."

She slid one chair over so he could sit down. She knew the ladies of the house would take her to task about it, but she feared a worse scene should she keep him standing there.

"I am asking you to dance with me."

"I suppose I cannot stop you from sitting in the chair next to me for a few minutes. But if it is rational conversation you seek, you will *not* get it from me on the dance floor." She blushed to the roots of her hair. "In these shoes I fear clumsiness. Please go ask someone else."

"I would enjoy sitting out the dance with you, but you know if I sit down, that spoiled charge of yours will come grab me with a pretext of some sort that starts with, 'Oh, my lord…'"

She smiled at his observation, wishing things could be different. He had certainly lost his antagonism toward her, but she knew he was not enjoying the party. She was probably the least objectionable person he could find. "That will be nothing to what you will hear should you stand up with her companion! I daresay she will swoon, too vexed to be so embarrassed."

"Kathryn, I do not tease you. The music is beginning, and I would like you to dance with me." He reached for her hand, but she shook her head no. He gently coaxed her from her seat, and Kathryn was caught in his eyes. Before she knew it, he was placing one hand on her waist. It was a waltz!

"Lord Dalton, I cannot. You do not understand. I am clumsy. I will embarrass you. Please…"

"Hush! You are doing admirably." Kathryn did not know what to do. All she dreamed about lately was being in his strong arms as she had been after the attack, sitting on a tree branch, safe from all harm. Now she was in his arms, and safe was the last thing she felt. She kept her head lowered, physically willing the big awkward shoes to move in the steps.

"Now, had I wished for a silent partner, I suppose that octogenarian across the room—I cannot recall her name—would have been happy to oblige me."

Kathryn could not credit the change in his manner. "*Mrs. Henry* would have been a far better choice, I assure you, and for more reasons than one."

She said the last a little more seriously. Charity would certainly ring a peal over her on the morrow. She looked down again, concentrating carefully on her steps. The waltz was her favorite dance, and she had not forgotten it. The shoes she wore, however, did not allow for graceful spinning around the dance floor.

He lifted her chin with their clasped hands. "Do you fear repercussions from your employer for dancing with me? Great guns! Why must everyone walk on eggshells around that girl?"

Kathryn actually did trip listening to the vehemence in his voice, but he quickly righted her in the steps without thought. "My lord, I am sorry if I led you to believe that. Charity will no doubt recount the tale for the next few days and continually mention that she had never been more embarrassed in her life." She smiled as she lowered her gaze, but only to his chest. "Charity's diatribes quite roll off my back."

"That relieves my mind excessively," he said, attempting to avoid another couple twirling by. Kathryn stumbled again.

They danced in silence for a few moments, but it was not awkward. At least not on her part. Outside of the shoes that made dancing almost impossible, it was too easy to remember their dances of such a long time ago. He may be merely acting polite, but for this moment she did not care.

"Kathryn," he said, and even her name on his lips felt completely familiar. "I suppose we should leave following breakfast in the morning?"

"Oh, dear, I had not thought about that. I must be sure to be gone before Charity and Lady Dinsmore are awake. They cannot know I am leaving the house the same time as you." She thought of something else. "I think no one must know it. The servants will surely talk about such things, and Lady Dinsmore's maid could tell her."

"How do you usually travel on your day off?"

"I do *not* travel, my lord, unless I wish to take Lacey and Jacob with me on an adventure. Sir John allows me the use of the pony cart or his carriage if he has no need of it. Otherwise, I walk and visit some of the tenants."

She saw a tic in his jaw and wondered if she had angered him again. "I suspect the ladies will sleep late after tonight. Do you suppose you would be able to eat breakfast at the least?"

"Yes, my lord."

"Then why do you not leave on foot in the direction you normally go, and I shall meet you where you tell me in my carriage."

"Very well." She would not look at him. "I am sorry if it will put you out."

"Shall we say nine of the clock, then?"

"Yes, thank you."

He seemed as intent on silence for the remainder of the dance as she. He appeared angry, but she was not sure if it was directed toward her. She had little time to think on it as her own thoughts crowded in.

Tomorrow was the day she would see her father. But even before that, she had to be sure she left the house unobtrusively. She would be mortified if anyone thought she was to spend her day off with Lord Dalton.

And what would they talk of during the drive? She feared a return of his antagonism or worse, awkward silence. But whatever the journey, her father waited at the end of it. Had she believed God heard her prayers, she would definitely have asked Him to allow a softening in her father's heart that might one day lead to a reconciliation.

As Lord Dalton returned her to her chair, his proper manners returned and he thanked her prettily for the dance and bowed low over her hand. She thought she heard him whisper that he looked forward to the morrow, but as Charity arrived to whisk him away, she could not be sure.

"Oh, Lord Dalton!" she interrupted with barely contained anger. "I knew you would never have left me a wallflower when it was you who specifically asked for this dance."

The self-centered chit sneered at Kathryn, as if saying she would be dealt with later. But she smiled adoringly up at him as she put her hand in his arm and curtsied.

The derision in her voice was patently obvious, and that she assumed the woman did not hear it or understand it infuriated Dalton. He was very close to ending his stay by telling the spoiled brat exactly what he thought of her! But he simply bowed to Kathryn and walked away on Charity's arm.

He had just learned she never left the manor, even on her half days. A pony cart, indeed! Lady Kathryn was *allowed* the pony cart! He was furious and afraid he had been curt with her at their parting.

Much later, Dalton sat in the darkened library nursing a glass of brandy and envisioning a bleak future. The brandy had barely been touched; he could not say the same for his heart. The party had been a dismal affair. To own the truth, he had been in no mood to put a false smile on his lips and be introduced as one of Charity's "dearest friends." He desired nothing more than to cut the girl directly, but he was a gentleman in *her* house so he kept a quiet tongue in his head and prayed for the evening to be over.

He was glad of Kathryn's presence there. He felt their connection and was saddened that the only time he was able to converse with her was the one time they danced.

So when the last guest departed and the family had taken to their beds, he remained in the library sipping his brandy as he paced in front of the fire. The movement allowed him to release nervous energy rising in him. He would take Kathryn to see her father, but he could not see clearly beyond that.

He was not even sure he wanted to see beyond that. They had silently and mutually declared a truce this evening. But was it only for *this* evening? He thought not, at least on his part. His mother had begged him not to become bitter, and he realized she was right. He only hurt himself each time he said something to crush Kathryn's spirit. Scripture said it best in Ephesians: *"Let all bitterness, and wrath, and anger, and clamor, and evil speaking, be put away from you, with all malice: and be ye kind one to another, tenderhearted, forgiving one another..."*

Tomorrow he must ask for her forgiveness. He imagined it would be a day they would not soon forget.

The next morning he picked up Kathryn, cloaked and hooded, in the lane in front of neat cottages. He got down to hand her into the carriage, climbed in after her and seated himself across from her.

She seemed reticent, almost *shy!*

She slowly lowered the hood of her cloak, and he felt as if the wind had been knocked out of him. She did not wear her disguise! He had never forgotten how beautiful she was, but she was a woman now. She took his breath away.

He could not imagine how all of the hardship she had lived through did not show on her face. But the sun that came through the windows to shine on her showed nothing but radiance. Her black hair fell in curls from a ribbon atop her head, and her skin was flawless. But her eyes—those remarkable sapphire eyes—were the windows into her soul. He saw the uncertainty in them, the fear of being exposed to him as herself.

He must not succumb to the desire to pull her into his arms and hold her as he had after her attack, before his world turned upside down and he recognized her. She must be made comfortable and allowed to savor the time with her father.

"Good morning, Kathryn. I am sorry you had to walk so far before I could take you up. Indeed, it makes me quite angry that you are not free to do as you please."

"My lord, if I am not angry about it, why should you be?"

"Because you will not be angry for yourself."

"It is of little import to me. I hereby free you from being angry *for* me!" She smiled. "What a silly conversation."

"It is not silly. I should be permitted to escort you somewhere on your day off. Openly! If others do not understand it, so be it."

She became very quiet. "It is not about you or me. It is about perception. How quickly you forget. If I were not already ruined, I would now be so. The only difference from the first time is that I am in your carriage."

He did not hear any sarcasm or anger, only the truth that he knew as well as she did, and its impact struck home. Had he not turned away in disgust only days ago when she told him she had eloped with Salford? That she had spent days in the carriage alone with him? *Lord, I have much to answer for.*

"I am sorry, Lord Dalton. I did not intend that the trip start out on such a note. I spoke without thinking."

"You must not apologize, Kathryn. I am so sorry for my words and actions on discovering your identity that night on the bridge. I am sorry for the circumstance that brought you to this place in your life." He ran his hand through his hair. "I have been too angry to see the woman who took the hardships life dealt you. And you not only survived, but became stronger because of them."

He saw the tears well in her eyes and thought of all the times they must have been there throughout her life, hidden by a pair of blue spectacles.

"I thank you for the kind words, my lord, but they are unnecessary."

"I assure you they are long overdue. I apologize for my behavior to you when I returned to Trotton. I have no excuse except for excessive pride."

"You said nothing I did not deserve. I do not hold that against you."

"No. What right have I to judge you or anyone else? That was only the most recent event in my life that I am not proud of. Had you known of the others, you might have planted me a facer for the way I treated you." He stared into her intense blue eyes, trying to emphasize his feelings. "I have asked for God's forgiveness, and now I seek yours."

"You have it, Lord Dalton. I think we need not discuss it any further."

She turned to view the passing landscape, but he could not look away from her. How could he have been so blind as to let a wig and spectacles hide her face from him? It was the face that haunted his dreams during battle. His anger and hurt had kept him from trusting, nay, loving another woman. Though the dreams had been nightmares, he remembered every inch of her face.

Two lives and nine years wasted in hurt and anger.

He let several miles pass in silence, but he finally had to ask her what tortured his heart. It might be the only opportunity he ever received. "Kathryn?"

She turned to him with a question in her eyes.

"May I ask you something?"

"Of course."

"You may tell me if you do not wish to talk about it."

She looked a little more wary, but answered, "Very well, my lord."

"Must we remain so formal?" He was stalling; he did not want to break the thin layer of their new relationship.

"I think so, sir. I go back to life as a companion. It took me long enough to lose the habit—I must not start it again."

He realized he did not have the slightest idea what that one decision on her part cost her. He would wait no longer.

"I wonder if you would tell me about…why Salford over me?"

Chapter Fourteen

She closed her eyes for one second, then opened them and turned back to the window. Of course he would want to know. Somehow it always came down to reliving the past, never moving on, and never settled. She would tell him, then she would never think on it again.

"It is not so…straightforward. Indeed, I did not choose him *over* you. Sometimes I think I did not *choose* him at all." She rubbed her furrowed brow. "No, that makes it sound as if I had no culpability. I chose to go with him of my own accord." She could not look at him as she relived this.

"Lord Dalton, I was young and stupid." She held up her hand to stop his denial. "That is not my defense. There is no defense for what I did. I only use my age as a sign of…inexperience." She realized she could not tell this story without explaining her feelings for him at that time, and she became embarrassed.

"Kathryn, I am sorry. I am being a boor, and you need not explain anything to me."

"I think it will be best if everything is out in the open. I know my father will certainly want explanations, so we will finish this.

"You were every girl's dream. You made me feel safe, and you made me feel important. But I never felt that you loved me. In truth, I sometimes felt I was the little sister you never had." She heard him groan. "I do not know how many times I may use inexperience as an excuse, but I thought two people just…knew." Her eyes welled up with tears again, but she hoped he could not see them.

"I know now that you must have been protecting my name from being bandied about. I felt you were feeding me sugar cubes as you did Jezebel, until I trusted you." The tears fell now. "I only knew I loved you."

"Kathryn…"

"No, I do not put any blame or any wrongdoing on you. How could I? I could only *know* what I was doing."

She wiped the tears off her cheeks; she was beyond caring what he saw or thought anymore. She just needed to get through the telling of it. "Lord Salford was introduced to me at a ball you did not attend. He seemed terribly old to me, but I thought him handsome and he paid me pretty compliments. I thought no more of it that night. The next time I saw him was at the opera, and as I look back, each time he…importuned me, you were not in attendance. Had I any brains, that would have spoken volumes to me."

Somehow the noise of the carriage and the horses disappeared as she went back in time, remembering it as though it were yesterday. "It was no more than two weeks before he began to declare himself in love with me. Sometimes he frightened me with his impassioned pleas, and then sometimes he was gentle."

She did not know whether to tell him this next part, but they were both adults now, and it might make him understand a little better. "I would sometimes mention you as I looked for you in a crowded room, and I know now that is when he realized he might have to go through you first. He began to point out the parties you did *not* come to as signs you did not really want to be with me. He asked if you ever told me I was more beautiful than any other." She laughed, a hysterical sound. "He said it ad nauseam, but I did not see it then.

"He said he would die without me. He asked if *you* ever told me that. I was young, but I knew right from wrong. I was tested and I failed. God has shown me that."

"Kathryn, what have I done?" He reached over to take her hands. "How could I have been so blind?"

"My lord, I knew on my first night alone, after he left me, that your feelings, whether love or not, were the more real and, therefore, the more worth having." She pulled her hands away to get her handkerchief from her reticule, to blow her nose and wipe her eyes. "It was too late by then. He convinced me that my father would not grant him permission to marry me." This time she actually laughed *at* herself. "Somehow, it never occurred to me to ask him myself!" She finally turned to look at him. "He convinced me to elope, and I knew it was wrong all the while. I got what I deserved. For a while after that, I wondered if I could have really loved you if I would let him tear me away. But life went on, and I realized I had no idea what *real* love was at seventeen."

She dabbed at her eyes once more then put the hand-kerchief away. "I do not blame you, I do not blame my father, and I am tired of the what-ifs. I can only wonder at how long it will take you, my father and…God to forgive me."

She knew he wanted to talk further, but she needed to focus her attention now on meeting with her father. "My lord, if you do not mind, I would like to rest a bit before we get home, to my father's."

"Kathryn, I will let this go for a time. You know what you saw and felt during that time. You do not know what I saw and felt. I cannot let it end here. I will not press you further today, however."

She turned her face back to the window, her heart engulfed in sadness.

She believed she had just driven away the only man she could love, *for the second time.* She knew now she loved him. A deep, all-encompassing and mature love. He had treated her as he did when he came back to Trotton out of hurt. She knew that, and he had put that time behind them. Asking for her forgiveness made her realize how much deeper this love was than any she felt when she was but a child.

But even should he forgive her for the past, she could not ruin him. Should she reappear, it would only dredge up the old scandal, and she would not put him through that.

As they got closer, she began to fear seeing her father again. Lord Dalton said that he wanted to see her, but even if his anger had abated over the years, would their relationship ever be as close? Would she ever be a big part of his life again? Would he forgive her if she pleaded with him?

Would she ever stop living in fear?

"Kathryn, I must warn you—that is to say, prepare you before we arrive."

"Prepare me for what?"

"Your father has been ill, Kathryn, for quite some time."

"Ill? Why did you not say so? What is his sickness?"

"I did not tell you before because he made me promise not to. He did not want you to visit him out of pity. Now that we are almost there, I can truthfully tell him you chose to accompany me."

"You are scaring me. What is wrong with him?"

"He had a particularly violent attack of the influenza more than a year ago. It moved into his lungs, giving him pneumonia. In his weakened state, he could not fight it off."

"How bad is it, my lord?"

"I cannot say, in all honesty. From what I saw, I do not believe his doctors were treating him urgently enough, but I do not know that for a fact. My main purpose in telling you is so that you will be prepared for the way he looks."

She bit her lip to keep it from trembling.

"He has lost weight and appears…frail, I suppose. I hope to see him somewhat improved, if he has begun to recover properly. Even then, however, he will not be as you remember him. And you must not forget, even were he in the best of health, he is nine years older, so he would be different in appearance."

"Thank you for telling me the truth." Another horrible result of her actions long ago. She would not think the worst; she could not without falling apart completely. If they were truly reuniting in forgiveness and apologies, she would show him the happiness she felt. She would not hurt him any more.

As they turned into the gate, a flood of memories came rushing back. She closed her eyes. *Father, I am taking You at Your word from now on. You will use both good and bad in my life. But I know You hear my petitions. Do not let him die. After all of the time we have missed, please give us the chance to love each other again.*

The coach stopped at the door, and Lord Dalton helped her out. The front door opened, and Kathryn smiled with pure joy. She ran and threw her arms around the staid butler, who did something he had never done before. He hugged her back.

"Oh, Donaldson, how good it is to see you."

The butler choked out his own, "Miss, you're a sight for sore eyes." Realizing his mistake, he bowed. "I mean, my lady."

"It can be Miss or Kathryn or anything you like, Donaldson!"

She noticed, as Lord Dalton handed him his hat and gloves, that the butler mumbled, "I'm sorry about your last visit, my lord. God bless you." Lord Dalton shook his hand. She heard him speaking low to the servant, but as scared as she was, she ran to the stairs and ascended to the upstairs bedchambers. She knocked on her father's door, and Hendrick opened it as Lord Dalton joined her.

"Oh, Hendrick, it is so good to see you. I am so glad you are taking care of him— I could not imagine a better person. Can I come in? May I see him now?"

"Kathryn," Lord Dalton whisperded, "I sent a note earlier saying we would be here today, but he may be resting or need some time to prepare…"

"It is quite all right, my lord. His Lordship is sitting up comfortably and is waiting to see you both. We don't know how to thank you, sir."

"Say no more. It was for all of us."

Kathryn wondered at the words, but could not take the time now to consider them. She preceded Lord Dalton into the room, but she stopped suddenly, afraid of what she might see. She felt Lord Dalton take her hand in his, and they approached the bed together. The windows were all open, and the room was flooded with the late-morning sun. As she approached, she saw him and could no longer hold back the tears. She ran to the bed and knelt at its side.

"Father, oh, Father," she cried, "I am so sorry." She grabbed the hand he held out to her. She kissed it and clasped it to her, crying now in earnest.

She noticed Lord Dalton speaking to Hendrick, then moving toward the door. She wanted him to stay there with her, but her father began to speak and she did not get the chance to call him back. Hendrick came up behind her with a chair, and she pulled it close to the bed. She thanked him with her smile.

"Kathryn, Kathryn, my beautiful Kathryn," her father wept. He could not stop saying her name, and they both were unable to manage any other words for several moments.

"Father," Kathryn said, when their emotions were better under control. "I have been such a disappointment to you. All you ever did was love me, and I stomped on it and hurt you." She could not look at him. She laid her forehead against their clasped hands. "I wished for you so often, Father. You will never know how often."

"Kathryn," her father said, pushing her face up with their entwined hands so he could look into her eyes. "Hasty words spoken in anger drove you away from me. I am so very sorry."

Lord Dalton had been correct. Her father was a shell of the man he had been the last time she had seen him. Her tears were a mixture of lost time and fear for his life. She wanted everything to be easy for him now. Nine years had slipped away, and she just shook her head.

"You must let me speak. I was such a fool. You took me to London and showered me with clothes and gifts to make me feel beautiful among all the other girls. I never appreciated it as I should have. I just accepted it all as my due, what a parent was supposed to give their child."

"My darling girl," he said, but she would not let him speak. He could forgive her or not, but he would know the whole truth, then he must get well.

"When Mother died, you and I began to share everything. Miss Mattingly helped me tell you things I thought were too personal to share with you. And you listened. You just held me when there was nothing to say, or you talked to me until I was comfortable again.

"But in London, I stopped sharing my new experiences with you, thinking I was all grown up. And I left you behind. I was stupid and young. I did not realize the love and guidance I had in you.

"Please," she pleaded, tear-filled eyes imploring him, "please say you forgive me. You never have to see me again, but please say you forgive me for the mess I have made of my life…and yours."

"I have loved you more than my own life since the day you were born, Kathryn. That has never changed. You were forgiven long ago, my love. I have missed you, too." He had to lay his head back against the pillow, but he did not stop looking at her. She threw off her cloak and lightly touched his forehead. She was relieved there was no fever. "You need to rest now."

"No, Kathryn, I have been resting all afternoon. Sometimes I just cannot catch my breath. It goes away much easier now."

She wanted him to be quiet and still his breathing for a few minutes, so she sat back down and put her head on his hand as she held it tightly. "Father, all I ever wanted was to please you. You were so sad when Mother died. She was so sweet and giving. I always wanted to be like her. Her gentle and quiet spirit filled us both with peace more times than I can remember."

She heard his quiet shushing sounds as he rubbed the back of her hair with his free hand.

"When she died, you started to teach me…oh, everything. You taught me how to treat the servants with respect and kindness, not just Miss Matty. And you taught me to ride, so I could be with you no matter where you were on the estate. As I got older, you helped me understand the running of an estate as well as a household. I learned everything from you, and I never once thanked you. I took you for granted."

She kissed his hand and the words just kept pouring out, as if from her very soul. "And then when we went to London, I wanted you to be proud of me, but I was young and immature, and for the first time in my life, I wanted to be popular." She lifted her face to his again, looking into eyes as blue as her own. "You never taught me that. You taught me to please God, and pay no attention to what others thought.

"But in London I was overwhelmed. It seemed everyone knew everyone else. I felt a little alone. And you gently guided me at the beginning, teaching me Town ways as you had country ways." She had stopped crying. She had been storing these words away for nine years. Kathryn wanted him to understand her feelings completely.

"I remember my first party and how you stayed by me when I was scared, and you knew when to shoo me on my way to meet friends my own age. And once that began, I pushed you to last place. I did not want all of my new friends to think I was a rustic. I was often afraid to be myself, though that is what you, and God, would have had me do instead of acting like a spoiled debutante. I lost sight of everything that was important to me for a while."

"Have you forgotten, my daughter, the night you came home from Vauxhall Gardens?" Her eyes opened wide and she thought back. "You came home and ran into my arms, telling me how wonderfully happy you were. We sat on the floor in front of the fireplace, and you recounted each detail. For the first time, you shared your feelings about Lord Dalton. Just because you lost sight of me did not mean I lost sight of you. I had eyes in my head, and I have known your heart since you were a baby. You glowed whenever you spoke of him, and I knew on that night you understood your first feelings of love. You shared that with me, Kathryn. You did not exclude me from what was important." He sighed. "Could I have been so remiss that you did not know how very proud I was of you?"

"I felt your love—I always did. But I did not appreciate it." He shook his head no on the pillow, but she stopped him. "Father, I know I did not, because I know now what it is to have lost it." She began looking past him. "I threw it all away. In my heart, I knew running away would make you unhappy, but I believed him, Father. If I had talked to you about it, I never would have listened to him. I am so sorry. I threw away everything you had ever given me with one decision, and I have regretted it every moment since it was made."

"My daughter, I am glad you have had your say." Silent tears rolled down the sides of his face. "You were my world. Did I never tell you? I suppose I did not. But I thought you knew that. And if I had told you that Lord Dalton wanted to marry you that night on the floor in front of the fire, I think you might never have had to make such a decision on your own. If nothing else, you would have decided knowing all the facts."

"Lord Dalton asked your permission to marry me?"

Her father lay back, his breathing more labored now. She would have to get that answer at a later time. Right now she prayed for the time to make peace with her father. "I love you with all my heart, Kathryn, and there is nothing to forgive. I have lived so many years in fear for you." It seemed he knew he would not be able to talk much longer. He was making every word count. So she began to tell him about her life at Dinsmore Manor so he would lie back and relax. She told him of Lacey and Jacob, and he smiled at her often.

"Now tell me how you are, Father, and always the truth. We are starting over." She tried to put every ounce of love into her smile.

"I will tell you, then, that I might not have been here today if not for Lord Dalton. Did he tell you about our visit? It was touch and go for me only last week. I feared I had few days left. But we spoke of you for hours. What a special, God-fearing man he is, Kathryn. I wish that for you."

She did not want to disappoint him on their first day together, so she led him away from that subject. "Father, I must go back to resign my position, but may I return? Will you let me care for you?" She did not tell him it would be in her disguise when necessary. She would no more sully his good name than she would…anyone's.

"My darling, this is your home. Our home. You belong here for a time, and I will never turn you away." He coughed, but it was not in distress; it was to clear his throat. "Kathryn, before we let go of the past, I need to know that you have come out of your…experiences all right. I did not know anything, though I searched and searched for you." He held her hand up to his cheek. "I do not know if Lord Dalton told me everything. I am sure he spared me details he thought might overpower me. But you need to give me your word that you have survived all that has happened to you." His voice broke. "I have worried for so long, and it seems I was right to."

"Father, the past is the past. We are starting over, remember?"

"I hope someday you will share that time of your life with me, but I will not press you today."

"The most important thing for you to know is that when there was no one else, Miss Matty was always there."

"I am forever in her debt. Do you think she will come here and allow me to thank her in person?"

"Father, that would be my greatest wish. I was hoping you might do something of a monetary nature for her. No amount could ever repay her for what she did for me, but I would like her to know she will never be in need of anything for the rest of her life. She will have her cottage and a nest egg, so she need not work any longer, and she would be available to visit us any time. Is that something you would do for her?"

"My girl, of course, of course. But more importantly, it is what you can do for her. You seem to have forgotten that you are wealthy in your own right. How I wished for some sign of you so I could get you back, never again to worry whether you had enough to eat."

"If that is still the case, then that is the first thing I will do. And Father, I wish to have Lacey and Jacob visit us when you are better. Would that be acceptable to you? I cannot lose them now."

"My darling, it is your home. You may do as you wish. It would be wonderful to have little ones around to keep me young. I wait longingly for the day you have your own."

She would not cry now! Knowing her future did not hold that blessing was so very hard, but she had her father back, and she would be able to watch Jacob and Lacey grow until they became tired of visiting her.

"I will let you rest, but I would know how your doctors are treating this. I know you will think me an interfering daughter, but I wish to nurse you when your doctors are not here."

"Did Dalton not tell you?"

"Tell me what?"

"Ah, the man is humble, as well. I should have expected that."

"I do not understand."

"Your Lord Dalton found me very near death. He promised he would bring you, but I honestly did not know if I would be here or not."

"Father…"

"I had to face the truth. I see Dalton shielded you from the worst."

"It seems he did. But I would guess, since he did not yet know the true state of things, he did not want me to think the worst." She loved him for that. "So what has wrought this improvement? Or do you shield me from it, as well?"

"No, my dear, no more. I knew I was dying. There did not seem to be anything to do but wait. Dalton had other ideas." He chuckled at the remembrance. "He cleaned house, to be sure!"

"Whatever do you mean?"

"He had Hendrick and Donaldson hopping! Asked them how I was supposed to breathe clean air when all of the windows were closed tight. He even complained about the curtains being closed. He wanted to know how my pallor would improve with no sunlight. They were shocked indeed, but by Jove, they did his bidding."

He turned a little more serious. "The next day, a gentleman arrived with a note from Lord Dalton. He asked permission for Dr. Walker, that was the gentleman, to house himself here and handle the overseeing of my treatment. He didn't believe the quacks handling my case were as informed about pneumonia as his man was." He lay back against the pillows again, and Kathryn could see the tiredness in his face.

"I have not felt this good in a long while, my child. It has only been a short time, but Dr. Walker tells me I can try getting up little by little over the next few weeks to see how I do. He thinks the more I do, the sooner I will get better."

"Father, I am so glad. But even I can see you are worn out. I have tired you. Now lie back and try to get some sleep."

"Will you leave now?"

"I must go back to Trotton to tell Lady Dinsmore

in person that I will be leaving her employ. I must go to them as they know me, so I will not bring notoriety to them in any way. And I must say goodbye to the children. But I will be home within a few days." She choked back tears. "I have only just found you. I will not lose you again."

"Please tell Lord Dalton thank you, if I am not to see him again today. He brought me back to life, and he brought you back to me. I am indebted to him."

"I will tell him. Now sleep."

Kathryn left the room slowly, almost afraid to stop looking at him. He would not die, because Lord Dalton had taken the time to care. When she opened the door to leave, his valet was there, ready to attend him.

"God bless you, Hendrick, for your loyalty and care of my father. It can never be repaid."

"It was Lord Dalton's doing, miss. Without Dr. Walker, I don't know where we'd be now."

"But you have been with him always. I cannot thank you enough. Do you think we can set up a meeting with Dr. Walker so I may introduce myself and find out how I can best help him?"

"Yes, my lady, whenever you say."

"Thank you, Hendrick. Thank all the staff for me, please. I can never repay you all for your loyalty to us these many years. Even when I was a little girl, I knew which of you might sneak me a treat or let me stay up later. I will never forget, I promise." Her heart was full. "I have learned something of a servant's lot over the past few years. You will never be servants again. You will always be part of the family."

"We have always felt part of the family, miss. Between your mother, father and you, we knew we were blessed to be here."

Kathryn hugged his neck. "I will return in a few days to take up residence again. Keep your watchful eye on him."

"Your return will be a joyous occasion, miss. For all of us."

"Hendrick, can I ask one more question before I leave you to my father? Do you know where I might find Lord Dalton?"

"He is in the green room, I believe."

How could she ever repay Lord Dalton for reuniting her with her father? Even more, how could she thank him for saving his life?

Chapter Fifteen

Kathryn's tears began to flow as she walked down the stairs to the green drawing room and she saw him standing by the fireplace looking into the flames. When he heard her he turned, and she walked straight into his arms, throwing her own around his neck. She knew he was surprised, but it did not stop him from wrapping his arms around her and holding her like he would never let go. She whispered in his ear, "Thank you, my lord. Thank you so much for everything. I am sorry I was so blue-deviled before. I have been so unhappy for so long."

He did not say anything. He just held her. She knew she had overstepped her bounds, but words were not enough.

She slowly pulled away from him, blushing as she straightened her gown, sure she had embarrassed him beyond measure.

"Let me fetch my cloak, and I will be ready to go when the carriage is brought around. I fear I have stayed

too long. It will get us back much later than I had intended."

A little while later, he handed her into the coach after
her tearful goodbyes to the servants. She leaned back
against the squabs, closing her eyes for a few moments.
She was emotionally spent, but happy.

He had not spoken since she had unabashedly thrown
herself at him. They rode along in silence for quite
some time. But there was something now that she must
know. She opened her eyes, and he sat staring at her in-
tensely with a furrowed brow. He had every right to be
displeased, but she supposed it would not matter when
she broached this subject.

"My lord?"

"Yes, Kathryn."

"You needed to ask me about Salford on our way
here—you needed to hear the truth from me." She
rushed on before he could say anything. "May I now
ask you a question?"

"Of course."

"Why did you not tell me you had asked my father's
permission to marry me in London?"

He let out an audible sigh, but she could not read his
expression to know what it meant. He was silent for a
few moments.

"Because I did not know how." He now put up his
hand to ward off *her* comments. "When I left Trotton
after discovering it was you, all I thought about was
my feelings. I was selfish and I was mean because I
still harbored such bitterness. It was easier for me to

believe I was the only one that suffered." He shook his head and muttered, "What a fool."

The carriage was in and out of the shadows now as late afternoon settled upon it. "When I walked away in anger, that was the only emotion I could latch onto. And while I was gone, I let that anger grow out of control until I wanted to hurt you as I had been hurt. That is when I made my decision to return to Dinsmore Manor. I cannot think about it without wondering at myself. I claim to be a godly man—even if I discovered you had hurt me on purpose, I should have been the one to turn the other cheek."

"My lord, we have been over this. It is in the past. You have apologized, and I have accepted that apology."

"Have you forgiven me, Kathryn? Or have you merely decided to accept the hands of fate and move on?"

"I do not know how to answer that. I fear my understanding of forgiveness has become somewhat cloudy over the past nine years. But that is beside the point. I do not blame you for your actions, so there is really nothing to forgive."

"I see." He ran his fingers through his hair in what she now recognized as a habit indicating frustration. She hated to see it.

"My lord, it is over and done with. Please forget I asked about it at all."

"I cannot. Since the night I tried to embarrass you at dinner, in front of the Dinsmores, I have been reminded—convicted by my own part in what happened to you. I have been trying to find the right time…the right words…to confess that action to you.

"But when you told me about Salford, when you told me how he convinced you I did not care for you, I do not know if I will ever be able to forgive myself."

He sat up straighter, and he spoke more forcefully. "When I talked to your father, I knew he must be concerned about how young you were. I thought to convince him of the sincerity of my feelings for you by moving slowly, giving you time to enjoy yourself and giving you time to get to know me. I hoped that by the end of the Season, you would choose me over anyone else you met."

This time she closed her eyes at the misunderstandings and cross-purposes that had played a part in that Season.

"If I had told you that I had talked to your father, that good-for-nothing Salford would never have been able to convince you I did not care." He barely stopped for breath. "Do you still think it was *you* who made the mistake? I came back to Trotton with vengeance in my heart, and I have learned that I played the major part in allowing the cur to do nothing short of abducting you."

"Lord Dalton—"

"No. I am glad your father told you. But I will never know if I would have been man enough to confess it on my own."

"Lord Dalton, I forgive you."

He wanted to believe her. By her own admission, her understanding of full forgiveness had been lost to her somewhere along the way. She felt that she did not deserve it because of what she had done. Then, accepting the fact that none would give it to *her,* she gave it freely to him.

He did believe her.

Later that night, Dalton sat in the library again at Dinsmore Manor, a half-filled glass of port sitting on the Queen Anne table next to him. He had not seen Kathryn after they returned home, and dinner had seemed interminable. He feigned fatigue when the tea table arrived in the drawing room, and he had waited, quietly reading his Bible until the house was silent before coming down to the library for a drink.

He was tired. This day had taken him through a gamut of emotions he hadn't even realized he was feeling.

They had not spoken again in the carriage. She had offered him forgiveness without a qualm. It touched him so much, he could not speak. He had made her suffer almost a fortnight before realizing he was no longer angry. And she gave forgiveness without question.

She made him drop her off at the lane where he had picked her up. He was tired of pretending. She had made up with her father. She was Lady Kathryn. But she would not listen. She did not wish to leave the Dinsmore family as anything other than Kate Montgomery. She had left her disguise in the gatehouse, and it seemed she donned it and went straight to her room upon their return. She did not even appear at dinner. Apparently, it was still her day off.

Thinking back now, he smiled as he kicked the coals

in the fireplace and watched them spark back to a warm glow. Today, for a few hours, she had been the carefree daughter of a marquis, a seventeen-year-old debutante, once again innocent and happy. She had hugged the butler and her father's valet, and he remembered things about her that he used to love. God's truth, he missed her.

He had no right to ask her about Salford, but not knowing was eating at him. When she discovered the blackguard had misled her, and made her think that *he* had never truly cared for her, any trace of anger she carried seemed to melt away.

But he had been a coward. He had not confessed the one thing that might have changed their history. He had gone to the drawing room while she was with her father and cried for the nine years they had all lost.

When he heard her enter, much later, she had come to him and thrown her arms around his neck. He had been surprised! But it only took him a moment to wrap her tightly in his arms, realizing she was right where she belonged, then and now, and he did not want to let go.

He loved her. Perhaps he had never stopped altogether. But he loved the Kathryn she had become much more than he had loved the young girl. She was not the fragile flower he needed to protect from every bad thing. She was a strong, confident woman who had braved too many of those already, and conquered them all.

She had scars from the battles, yet she was able to fall in love with two small children—probably many more in her career—with her whole heart and soul, withholding nothing for fear of being hurt again. She had allowed him to come back into her life, vengeance making him cruel, until he got too close to hurting people she cared about.

And when she brought to light his part in the tragedy that had become her life, forcing him to confess it, she freely gave him what he needed—her forgiveness. He could not speak after that. He only wanted to ask her one thing, but he was too afraid of her answer.

He wanted to marry her.

He had to be realistic. She *had* come into his arms, but she had also hugged the butler! She was happy. So completely happy that she forgave and forgot nine years of unmitigated pain. And though she had forgiven him, he did not know if she cared for him. He did not know if she loved him, had ever loved him. He had been so busy wrapping her in cotton, she had left with another man.

He closed his eyes against the weariness and the melancholy. Only seconds later he heard the dreaded word…

"Fire!"

Kathryn sat at her dressing table, staring in the mirror at the strange creature reflected there. She had remained dressed, too drained to change, and had fallen asleep. The house was quiet now, and she lit the candle by her bed. She reached down, removed her shoes and rubbed her sore feet. She sat up and began pulling the pins from her hair to remove the offending wig. Her own hair fell about her shoulders, and she sighed in relief. Taking her spectacles off, she lay back on her bed fully clothed.

The tears rolled out of the corners of her eyes. She had been reunited with her father today! For the first time in nine years, she was joyful. Yet she let despair creep in because she now wanted the one thing she could never have. She loved Lord Dalton with her whole heart and soul, for the second time in her life.

She would probably never see him again; he had not said a word in the carriage after she told him she did not blame him for what had happened. She just wanted the past to be the past. She did not see him once they returned to the house, and he would be leaving in the morning.

Charity would rant and rave about the way each of them had interfered in her plans, and would use them both as an excuse for not catching him. And in her case, Charity would be right. Kathryn had quite a bit to answer for—another blot on her soul that God would not forgive.

She sat up on the bed and seemed vaguely aware of heaviness in the air, her lone candle shrouded in grayness. An acrid smell of smoke reached her. Going immediately to the fireplace, she could tell that the smoke did not come from there. She took her candle and turned to open the door to her room. A piercing scream she was likely never to forget rent the air with one word....

"Fire!"

The surprise of the scream made her jump, causing her candle to go out, but that did not stop her immediate dash into the hallway. She thought she recognized the scream as belonging to Sally, and that could only mean the fire was in the vicinity of the nursery. She did not know Sally well enough to guess a flair for the dramatic, so without further thought, she put down the useless taper and ran from the room.

The thick smoke washed over her immediately, causing her to cough as her lungs filled with the black cloud and her eyes burned in irritation. She pulled the sleeve of her dress up to cover her mouth and nose and ran to the nursery door at the end of the hall. The knob was warm to the touch, but she opened it and froze at the sight of the flames billowing out of the small book room off the main nursery chamber.

Sally appeared behind her carrying Lacey, who was crying in her arms. She grabbed at Kathryn's gown. "Come, Miss Montgomery, we must get out and warn the family on the floors below. Maybe the stable hands can get water up here before too much of the house burns." She tugged again. "We must hurry, miss."

"Jacob!" Kathryn screamed as the flames crackled and the smoke thickened. "Where is Jacob?"

"He weren't in his bed. He's more 'n likely already downstairs. Come, miss, we must go now."

"No, you go. Get Lacey to safety and warn the others." Kathryn coughed, as talking made her take in the smoke even with her mouth covered. "There was no time for him to run. I was in the hall immediately."

Sally began to cry. "He can't be in there, miss. Nobody could…be in there."

"Go! I must be sure." The tears that flowed at the fear she felt at Sally's words hindered her sight even more.

Kathryn called Jacob's name over and over, terror at the thought of him still being in the nursery making her hysterical. The actual blaze appeared to be confined to the small book room where they had built his Martello Tower, but flames licked the top of the door frame and would soon catch on to the curtains and wooden panels of the larger room she was in now.

There was nowhere in the nursery Jacob could hide, so she must check the book room. The smoke was now making it difficult to breathe at all, and she could only see the floor clearly.

Running to grab Lacey's doll blanket in the corner, she quickly drenched it in the water basin and made a tent around her head, hoping the smoke could not penetrate the damp cloth as quickly. She also knew she was as flammable as the nursery curtains, should stray embers catch her dress or hair.

Going to the door, she jumped back as the heat from the room overpowered her. No one could be alive in there. *God,* she pleaded, *please let Jacob be downstairs.* But she would not leave until she knew.

Sinking to the floor on her hands and knees, the smoke seemed less dense. She crawled through the doorway and screamed as the wall immediately to her left began to collapse in full flame. She dropped to the floor and rolled to her right. Nothing fell on her, but she now knew the doorway was partially blocked.

It was then that she saw him.

Jacob was huddled in the nearest corner, eyes wide in shock, his fear paralyzing him.

"Kathryn, where are you?" She heard the voices in

the nursery and prayed they would all make it out alive. No doubt she would now be the cause of someone's death as they came to *her* aid.

"I am here!" she screamed at the top of her lungs. "I am all right." She thought she heard Lord Dalton giving the same exclamation she had when she first saw the book room from the nursery. She wanted to keep them away. "Stay back," she coughed out. "Jacob, must get Jacob," was all she could say at the last, and she crawled to the terrorized child, trying with all her might to soothe him with words through a parched and burning throat.

He did not seem to hear her, so she took the soaked blanket from around her head and wrapped his shaking body in it as completely as she could. She knew she could not carry him out on her hands and knees, but standing meant any one of those flames could be upon her in seconds. She began to wring as much of the excess water out of the blanket and onto her clothes as she could.

"Here we go, Jacob, love. We are going to run out of here as fast as my legs will carry us." She put her feet under her, but stayed crouched and lifted the little boy into her arms.

"Kathryn," she heard from the nursery. "Get out of there, now!"

She knew Lord Dalton's voice even through the crackling of the fire and the crumbling of the wood around her. And she had to admit that even amidst the biggest battle of her life, she knew a hysterical desire to laugh at him and ask him what in the world he thought she was *trying* to do!

"On the count of three now, Jake. You count with me. One, two, threeeee!" she screamed, stood and ran through the blazing doorway of the book room at full force into another body, who "oomphed" as she knocked the wind out of him. That same body she had run to when she was attacked on the bridge, and the same arms that had wrapped around her earlier in the day. He immediately pulled her to the ground and soaked them with the rest of the water in the basin.

Kathryn, still holding Jacob, was then lifted into strong arms and carried out of the smoke-filled nursery, which seemed filled with people.

As her rescuer carried her down the hall, she finally reached a point free enough of the smoke where she could see all of the Dinsmore servants lined up. They were passing buckets of water, man to man, down the hallway to the nursery. She was sure the lead man in the nursery must come out as he emptied his bucket, as it would be impossible for any one person to stay in that room for very long.

Kathryn felt water running down her neck and back, and it was the greatest feeling she had ever known. She was not lost to her senses despite watering eyes and no voice, and though she thought she could have walked, she was happy to be in Lord Dalton's protective arms, finally feeling that she and Jacob were safe.

She leaned into him, closed her burning eyes and pulled Jacob closer to her, trying to get in greater gulps of air and letting Lord Dalton take her where he would.

She found she was suddenly very dizzy, and so thirsty she would share a bucket of water with one of Lord Dinsmore's horses if that was all that was available to her.

"Stupid," she heard rumble through the chest conveniently pressed against her heart. "Stupid, brave girl."

Kathryn smiled to herself and snuggled closer. It was not *precisely* a compliment, but she would take it nonetheless. Her eyes suddenly jerked open as she heard Lady Dinsmore scream in ragged tears, "My baby, my baby!" Sir John took Jacob from her wet grasp, causing a slight shiver as she became bereft of his body warmth.

"Oh, Miss Montgomery, is he well? How can I ever thank you?" Her hysteria increased with each word. "Sally told us you would not leave until you found him. God bless you Kate, again and again."

Kathryn barely felt a warm, dry blanket being put around her shoulders and heard from far away Lord Dalton ask her if she thought she could stand.

"I believe so.... I do not know," she croaked, and he gently touched her bare feet to the floor, holding on tightly until she was sure her legs would hold her. As soon as Lord Dalton tried to wrap her in a warm blanket, her knees buckled and he lifted her once again into his arms.

It appeared they were in the room where the party was held. She could not think why, even when she heard through a fog that it was the farthest room from the nursery. It seemed the fire was contained at the end of the third floor. A glass was placed against her lips, and a large shoulder lifted her head to receive the coolest liquid she could ever remember gliding down her parched throat. She sighed in total contentment.

As the drink continued in small doses, she heard, "Not too much at one time—your stomach is probably lined, as well."

It was then she realized the entire household was present, and it was very quiet. It seemed every eye in the room was trained on her.

What were they staring at?

Then Kathryn did something she had never done before. She fainted.

Chapter Sixteen

Kathryn slowly opened her eyes to the sting of lingering irritation, and to sunlight that seemed extremely out of character with the condition of the world. She was in a bed, alone in a guest chamber. She did not remember anything after her knees gave way, so she must have been carried here...perhaps by Lord Dalton?

She was surprised when the door opened and two heads peeped in like baby birds above a nest's edge. "Can we come in, Miss Montgomery?" asked a timid Lacey, for some reason unsure what the response would be.

Katherine knew she was not prepared for the visit. Her body screamed in several places as she tried to sit up in bed, but she could not bring herself to send them away. Indeed, they must feel quite left out, if the previous treatment of their worries was any indication.

"Of course you may," she said, sitting up and realizing her wet dress had been removed, and someone had wrapped a warm robe around her. "I am afraid I was a little unwell last night, so I must have been allowed to sleep in. I am glad you have come to keep me from becoming a slugabed."

At her words, Jacob began to cry, and Kathryn hurriedly bundled him into her arms as she carried him to a brocade settee, Lacey close behind.

"Hush, Jacob," Kathryn whispered, calming him. "You two have never been to visit me before breakfast, and I own to being a bit surprised. Are you still scared about the fire last night? You must not be, you know. Everything will be determined safe before you will be allowed to return upstairs."

"It's all my fault, all my fault," he sobbed. Kathryn peeked over his head to Lacey, seeking answers in her eyes. Lacey only lowered her own. "Sally told me… well, she didn't tell *me,* I heard her tell the footman, but it makes no never mind. It's still my fault." Jacob could not continue, his sobs overcoming him again. She only held him tighter and turned to Lacey.

"Sweetheart, you must know what is troubling him. Can you not tell me?"

Lacey nodded her head, but seemed wary of speaking.

"Darling, you know you may say anything to me, whatever is on your mind."

"You might be angry, Miss Montgomery. You might be as mad at us as everyone else is. When Sally came to take us outside a little while ago, we heard her tell James that she was to keep us out of Papa's sight or we would get a rare trimming."

"What is this all about?" Kathryn asked. It was hard

to hide the anger in her voice. Her heart felt their lone-liness, and she would not let them be treated this way. "Tell me what is upsetting your father so much that it has him in such a taking?"

"Some men have been in the nursery all morning. We knew it would need to be fixed some, but these men were not the ones who would be fixing it. They asked us questions and questions about last night and…and they say it was Jake who caused the fire." Lacey auto-matically rubbed her brother's back in comfort. "Papa says he can't even punish Jake until his steam runs out, or something like that."

Kathryn was livid. Sir John and Lady Dinsmore al-most lost their son last night. Their son and heir! Lady Dinsmore had been hysterical until she could take Jacob from her arms last night. Yet today they were angry enough to completely isolate them? These children had been traumatized, as well. Where was the love and con-cern for them?

What was she thinking? They had never given them love and concern.

Now she had to try to control her temper so she could calm them.

"Jacob, you must not cry any longer," Kathryn said in a sterner voice. He seemed to understand her sever-ity did not necessarily mean anger. "Tell me why they think it was you. I shall not be upset with you, only tell me what happened."

"It *was* me, Miss Montgomery." Jacob hung his head and said his next words in a quiet voice. "It was me." He paused for a moment. "I 'fessed it to them like you told me I should always do if I do something bad." He heaved a few gulps of air and began to tear up, but went on. "Only they didn't say I did a good thing to tell them like you do. Everyone yelled at me, and Charity said I should be shipped away to school." He cried in earnest at those words. "Don't let them ship me away, Miss Montgomery, please?"

"Jacob, you know your sister flies into the boughs sometimes and says things she does not truly mean." Kathryn's soothing voice was having its effect on Jacob's hysterics as he thought about her words. "Now tell me what you confessed."

"I woke up and couldn't sleep, so I was thinking about how to finish my moat. I had a grand idea to put in a drawbridge, and I wanted to see if it would go over the water. I took Sally's candle with me. She had fallen asleep in the chair, you see." He began to whimper as the memory came back to him. "I was only going to be a minute, I was gonna put it right back, but when I set it on the floor, I must of put it too close to the pile of blue stuff for the water. It happened so fast, Miss Montgomery."

Kathryn's goal now was to quell his fears as he remembered each detail. She kissed the top of his head and said, "You must have been very scared, Jacob. What happened next?"

"I tried to blow it out, but it just seemed to get bigger." Tears rolled freely down his face. "When it burned my tower, I cried, but it climbed up the wall. I ran to the other side of the room to get away from it. Then you found me."

Kathryn now cried with him. She hugged him so tightly he squeaked. When she thought of what could have happened to him, she shuddered. *God, I know You are angry with me, but thank You for taking care of this special boy.* She could not stop her tears, hoping God knew how sincere she was.

"Jacob, it happened because of something you did, but it was an accident. You have been told that you must not touch the candles and that is why—they can be so very dangerous. Now your father is exceedingly angry, and you must be punished." She added another silent prayer that Sir John would not take his anger out on the boy. "I have told you we all must be responsible for our actions, and though he will punish you, he is probably more upset when he thinks about what could have happened to you." She knew she was being generous, but she could not allow Jacob to live the rest of his life traumatized over this one mistake, costly as it could have been. She knew only too well how a heart hindered by the past could become colder as the future loomed before it.

"But I almost got you hurt, Miss Montgomery," Jacob cried, touching her heart. "I would never do anything to hurt people, 'specially you, honest I wouldn't."

Kathryn hugged him once again. "I know, love, and I am not angry with you, Jacob. I am only fearful when I think of how *you* could have been hurt. We must be thankful it was only wood and furniture that were damaged. And we must tell God that tonight in our prayers." Though she was at outs with God, she would help these children know Him, just as Miss Matty had done for her.

She pulled Lacey to her and held them both in silence for a few moments with a déjà vu feeling of just the same being done for her less than a fortnight ago. She then heard another knock on her door and called, "Come in," over the children's heads.

"Um…Miss Montgomery…Lady Dinsmore wishes to see you in the drawing room. Oh, and Lord Dalton asks to speak with you at your convenience, if you are up to it." Kathryn thanked the servant and told her she would be down as soon as she was dressed. Of a sudden, she realized she was not wearing her spectacles, and she reached up to discover she was no longer bewigged. She closed her eyes as the weight of what really happened would change everything.

No wonder all eyes had been upon her when Lord Dalton carried her into the dining room. They either had no idea who she was, because Lord Dalton kept calling her Kathryn, or they were confused that Lady Dinsmore *did* know who she was and was calling her Kate.

What were the children thinking? They had no problem recognizing her, though her appearance was different. She would need to explain it to them later. Later when she must tell them goodbye. No, she could not think about that now.

She smiled her loveliest at Jacob and tweaked his chin. "You two scamps need to go outside as Sally asked you. Now, be as good as gold and do not give her any need to scold you on your behavior." Her smile belied the panic inside her.

Both children walked away quietly, and it seemed to Kathryn that they had been *somewhat* relieved at her reassuring words. Lacey curtsied, trying ever so hard to be grown-up. She seemed to remember something she wanted to say as she rose to leave. "You look very pretty in the morning when you wake up, Miss Montgomery." Taking Jacob's hand, she smiled once more at her beloved idol, and they left the room sedately so a reprimand would not be needed.

The second the door closed behind them, Kathryn covered her face with her hands. She had intended to resign today, but all she wanted was to leave as Miss Montgomery. Seems she had allowed herself to be too happy.

Her eyes filled with tears. She ran to her room, barely minding her way. She must get through these two interviews. Then she would pack and go home. Her father awaited her there.

She donned the dress she used on her midnight walks and tied her hair back in a ribbon. She had no time for more.

Kathryn knocked on the drawing room door and opened it at the response to come in. She entered the room to find Lady Dinsmore its sole occupant.

"Do come in, Kate," Lady Dinsmore's voice commanded from the love seat. "It is Kate, is it not?" Of course she would want a full explanation.

"Actually, it is Kathryn, my lady, but I will always be Kate to you."

"No matter what the explanation, Kate, I do not know how to thank you for rescuing my son from the fire." Real tears rolled down her cheeks. "We surely would have lost him had you not gone back into the burning room. I am indebted to you." With that, she rose and hugged Kathryn and would not let go until she was cried out.

Kathryn held her until she gathered some semblance of control, then helped her back to the settee. Kathryn sat in a chair across from her. "Ma'am, I do not deserve your thanks. It is what anyone would have done. But pray, could you use your influence with Sir John to treat Jacob…carefully?"

"My dear Kate, still worrying over the little ones. It is just like you." She pulled a handkerchief out of her sleeve and blew her nose. "I will not deny that he is prodigiously angry with him. But it will burn out very soon, as it usually does." She rose again and began pacing the room.

"What is it, my lady?"

"Will you explain to me now, please, who you really are and why you have been masquerading in such a fashion?" Kathryn did not think she was angry, more befuddled.

"Lord Dalton did not tell you, ma'am?"

"Oh, dear, is Lord Dalton aware of this? Perhaps I should ask Sir John to come in, as well."

"That really will not be necessary, Lady Dinsmore. I know his presence sometimes oversets you. I believe I can explain to your satisfaction." She rose from her chair and began to pace. "Lord Dalton recognized me from when I was in London. I thought he might have given you my name or…what it is he remembers from so long ago." This was not as easy as she first thought. She asked if she could sit down again, and Lady Dinsmore nodded her assent.

"After my London Season, circumstances occurred requiring me to make a living on my own. I applied for many positions, but was always told I was too young and that my appearance would be a temptation to the men of the household."

"Because you are so beautiful," said Lady Dinsmore. It was a statement, not a question.

Kathryn stood again, writhing her hands. "I have always hated that word. I accept the fact that I am passable, but I was naive and did not realize… It makes no difference now. I had to come up with a way I could hide my appearance. As you know, I held two very successful positions before I came to you."

"That does not explain why you did not reveal this to me when I hired you."

"My lady, I did not wish to put you in the position of living this lie with me. I did not wish to ever be recognized by anyone among the *ton,* but if *you* knew, it would have made it difficult for you to keep my secret, and it would have been humiliating for me."

"I see. I owe you a debt for saving my son's life, but what are we to do now?"

"I will give you my notice today. We must admit that Charity has no need of a companion. She will do as she wishes, and I believe that she will be a success when you take her to Town, despite our…concerns."

"Let us not be hasty, Kate…Kathryn. I had no plans

to terminate your employment—I just wished to know the truth."

"You have been so much more than kind to me, Lady Dinsmore. But I cannot stay. The decision was made yesterday, even before my identity came to light. I wished, however, to resign as Miss Montgomery, but I would have resigned in any event."

Lady Dinsmore became anxious. "Kate, you must stay. Indeed, I know you will stay when I tell you our plans. Sir John is exceedingly angry with Charity and her inability to capture the earl. He says he washes his hands of her, and I may take her to Town immediately for *this* Season! I have not told her yet. I wanted to be sure you would remain…but in a different capacity. We want you to be Lacey and Jacob's governess."

The tears welled up in Kathryn's eyes as she realized, once again, the unfortunate timing of circumstances in her life. "My lady," she said, tears overflowing now. "I am more sorry than you will ever know that I must decline your offer."

"No, you cannot. You may wear your trappings. We can raise your income. Please, Kate…Kathryn." Now she began to cry. "You must stay."

"Lady Dinsmore, my father is very ill, and I wish to take care of him. You must know I love those children as I would my own. I would not turn it down for any other reason, I promise you."

"Oh, dear, what shall we do?" she asked, waving her handkerchief. "Is there nothing I can say?"

"I am afraid not, my lady. But please know how

grateful I am to you for the past four months. I am indebted to you."

Lady Dinsmore hugged her, mumbling her goodbyes through tears. "You will say goodbye to the children?"

"Of course, Lady Dinsmore. I want you to know that I want to be a part of their lives if you will let me. Perhaps they can come for visits to my father's house? I do not want to lose them."

"I will talk to Sir John. It is very disconcerting. How will we explain your changed appearance?"

"They have already seen me and did not even question it. But if they do, I will tell them myself. Thank you, Lady Dinsmore, for everything." They clung to each other, knowing when they let go all would be changed.

"May I ask if you know where I might find Lord Dalton?" Kathryn asked. "He sent Sally to let me know he wished to see me before he left this morning."

"I believe he is with the baron in the stables. Perhaps Jarvis knows. Oh, dear, how am I to get Charity to pack and do all of the necessary things for this without you?" She put her handkerchief up to her mouth and ran from the room.

Kathryn had two more interviews before she left, and she did not know how she would survive either.

Tears came to Kathryn's eyes at the real distress in Lady Dinsmore's goodbye. Though the last was all about Charity, she understood the backhanded compliment the lady gave her in expressing her concern for the future.

Kathryn spoke the truth when she thanked the lady

for her kindness to her. Kathryn was treated with respect by every member of the household, excepting one, and it was not in the usual way of things for a companion to be treated almost as a member of the family, albeit a lower connection.

But she could not think on it for long. There were still two goodbyes to get through, and she dreaded them both.

Those two children meant the world to her. They were the joyous spot in every day for the past four months, and unlike Charity, they needed her. But though she would choose them over almost anyone else in her life, she could not do so to her father. She would be starting a new life together with him, and she thanked God for the reunion that brought them back together.

And Lord Dalton…she must let go of him again. She was glad they had made their peace; she would not put it past him to visit her father from time to time. She did not know which would be harder, saying goodbye forever, or saying goodbye and living for his next visit.

The loneliness had already begun to seep into her soul, and she was not even gone.

Chapter Seventeen

It was more excruciating than she could have imagined.

Kathryn walked quickly toward the lake, blushing at each servant's wide-eyed stare, but more worried about her goodbyes to the children. She must be strong, for them.

She saw where they played under the watchful eyes of Sally. She did not interrupt them for a while, but they seemed...restrained somehow. Tears filled her eyes. She knew that this was the last time she would see them in the foreseeable future. She no longer believed God was punishing her. She believed He had given up on her.

She came out of her reverie as she heard her name screamed by the two as they realized she was there. She dropped down to her knees to take one in each arm. She buried her head on their shoulders and cried silent tears of joy and pain.

"Miss Montgomery, Miss Montgomery, am I going to be sent away?" Jacob asked in one ear. She heard Lacey crying in the other.

She put them at arm's length and stared at them long and hard, burning their faces into her mind. She finally smiled and tousled Jacob's hair. "Jacob, I have asked your mother to be sure that will not happen."

Lacey remained quiet. Kathryn felt her reticence and decided she would talk to her first. But she wanted to do it alone. "Jacob, would you do me a huge favor? Would you go pick some of those wildflowers for me?"

Sally took his hand. "I'll take him, miss."

"Thank you," she said to the only real friend she had in the house.

Kathryn turned her attention to Lacey. She sat back on the ground and took the girl on her lap. She was too big for that now, but both of them needed it. "Are you unhappy, Lacey?"

The little girl nodded against Kathryn's shoulder. She must keep the quivering from her voice. "Do you want to tell me about it?"

She did not speak immediately, but her eyes welled up with tears. "Everything seems different. You look different, and Charity is very mean. Mama and Papa have not even spoken to us today." She threw her arms around Kathryn's neck and sobbed. With that, her broken heart was complete.

"Lacey, darling, your papa and mama are extra busy this morning. It is a very big secret so you must promise not to tell, but Charity is to go to London very soon, and they are making all of the arrangements. And your papa must also get the work started on the nursery." She rocked the girl gently.

"And you, Miss Montgomery? Are you to stay with us or go to London with Charity?"

It was too hard, Kathryn thought, but she would do this for them. "No Lacey, I cannot stay. I cannot stay here, and I will not be going to London." The young girl held her tighter, crying quietly. "It is no one's fault, Lacey. You noticed that I look different today. I want to try to explain it to you." How could she ever make this easy enough for a child to understand?

"I have told a sort-of lie, as I have told you *not* to do. My father and I had a very big fight once. We hurt each other, and I was very young and foolish."

The little girl was calmer now, but she still held tightly to Kathryn's neck. "I never wanted him to find me, so I changed my hair and wore spectacles. I stayed away from places he might be, so we would not meet.

"But Lord Dalton recognized me when he came. We were friends in London. He has helped me see that it was all a misunderstanding, and took me to see my father yesterday. We are both very sorry for our angry fight, and we forgave each other."

She rubbed Lacey's back and rocked her in her arms. "But he is sick, and I must care for him. I must go and stay with my papa. Do you understand?"

The little girl shook her head no.

"Oh, my darling Lacey. I will miss you so very much. But only because I will not be able to see the wonderful ways you grow every day. I will write to you each week, and you must write back to me. And when you get a little older you can come visit me. Would you like that?" She swallowed back her own tears.

Jacob ran up to them with the flowers, Sally not far behind. "Why do you still cry? Is it silly girl things?"

Lacey let go of Kathryn and stood up. "No, Jacob. Miss Montgomery came to say goodbye."

"Say goodbye? Till when?"

What had she done to these children? More than their parents' neglect had done, she was certain.

"Jacob, I must go be with my father. He is sick and has need of me."

"No, we need you," he said, and threw the flowers to the ground. He started to cry and ran to Sally. Lacey joined him there.

She knew they needed to withdraw from her to protect themselves. But they took the rest of her heart with them. "I need you, too, Jacob." Her voice broke. "But I must make a hard decision. You have Sally, but my father has no one except me." She raised her eyes to Sally, both of them tearing up as Kathryn passed the silent message to love them—love them with all of her heart.

Sally took over. "We must not let Miss Montgomery leave with tears. She wants to see your smilin' faces before she goes. Now go give her a hug."

Jacob ran to her and almost knocked her backward with the force of his body. She hugged him tightly and buried her face in his hair. "You will write me back, won't you Jake? We can share everything in letters. All right?" He nodded, but he could not speak.

"Master Jacob, let Miss Lacey have her say now."

Lacey walked up to her, but did not touch her or look at her. It was almost harder than tears. "Lacey, I need you to listen to me. I am not abandoning you. I love you too much. I promise to write every week whether you wish to write me back or not."

Kathryn was not going to be able to take much more. "You must not close your heart for fear of being hurt. Sally loves you, your parents love you and I love you. Jacob needs you. Other people will come into your life that will love you, too. And you must love them back with all of your heart, because that is what you do best."

Lacey ran to her and held on for dear life. Kathryn could no longer hold back her tears. "And when you have questions or problems, you write and let me know. Tell me your fears and your joys and it will soon feel better, like we are still together. Promise me, Lacey. I need you in my life, even if only this way for a while."

She nodded against Kathryn's shoulder. She held her away. "Lacey, tell me. You must not be afraid or shy again. Tell me, Lacey."

The girl fell back into Kathryn's arms and said in a choked voice, "I promise."

Sally let go of Jacob and he ran to them, crying, as Kathryn pulled him in with one arm. They remained that way for a few moments until Sally knew that none of them should cry anymore.

"Come children, we will go see if Cook needs our help for lunch. Say goodbye to Miss so she can help her father."

Kathryn whispered in their ears, "I love you both more than anything. More than anything. If you have need of me, just write. I promise I will come to you, and I will help you any way that I can. I love you."

She let Sally take the hand of each one and lead them

toward the house. Both looked back with the saddest faces she had ever seen, and she gave them a tremulous smile before they disappeared inside. She sat there for half an hour, crying as she stared into nothingness.

That is where Lord Dalton found her.

"Kathryn?"

He watched her turn away and quickly wipe the tears from her face. "Lord Dalton, I'm sorry, I know you wished to see me, but I had to—" she choked up "—to say goodbye to the children first."

He sat down next to her, and without thought took her into his arms, her head resting on his chest. She broke down again, and he did what he had done the night on the bridge, he held her, he rocked her and, with his chin resting atop her head, he told her everything was going to be all right. He let her have her cry.

She quieted after a few moments but did not remove herself from his arms. "I have broken their hearts. They expect that from everyone else, but not from me, and I just betrayed their trust." He felt a tear fall on his hand.

"Kathryn, I have no doubt you told them the truth. Children are inexplicably able to feel a lie. Their hearts are heavy, and they cannot understand all the actions of adults, but they know who they can trust. They trust *you*."

He stroked her hair. "Did you tell them you would see them again?" She nodded her head against his chest. "Then I know you will move mountains to make that happen." She nodded again.

Suddenly she pulled away from him and blew her

nose with her handkerchief. "I am sorry." She straightened her skirt and retied the ribbon, keeping her hair bound.

"What are you sorry for, Kathryn?"

She blushed. "You know what I am sorry for…for falling apart in your… You know what for," she said, wiping the tears from her eyes.

"You are correct—I do know *what* you are sorry for. I do not, however, know why."

She turned to look him in the face. He was so handsome and so strong. She was already leaning on him too much. She must remain strong on her own. "Why? Because I put you in an awkward situation? You would never have left me sitting here crying. I am sorry you felt the necessity of having to comfort me."

"I'm not. Can you really have been so engrossed in your father and the children that you do not see the change in me?"

"There has been no change in you. You have always been the kindest man I know."

"I see. When I tried to humiliate you in front of this family, I was being kind?"

"You were hurt. And I deserved your condemnation. It was not long before the kindest man I know was reuniting me with my father."

He leaned one arm on his raised knee and ran his fingers through his hair. "Kathryn, I know the timing is bad, but I cannot wait for another opportunity. Tell me you know it is not just kindness. Tell me you have noticed my newfound feelings for you."

She tried to rise, but he kept a strong hand on her arm. "No more running away."

"I must catch the stage to Montgomery Hall, and I am risking too much by remaining here without my disguise. I must go."

He waved his hand in the air. "My carriage will take you to your father when you wish it." Then he looked at her with a frown. "What is this about the disguise? We shall throw it into the lake there and wish it good riddance!"

She stared back at him in surprise. He feared he would not like her next words.

"I shall need the disguise, or some version of it for the rest of my life."

He was right. He did not like her words.

"But it is out in the open now—why continue it?"

"It is not all out in the open. You, my father and Lady Dinsmore are the only ones who know. I have asked Lady Dinsmore to keep my secret, and she has promised."

"I still do not understand. You are going to be with your father. You certainly do not need the costume while you are with him. Indeed, I do not see why you need it at all." He could feel himself getting angry, but he tried to stay calm.

"Perhaps not all the time." She stopped and sighed. "But should he have visitors, I will only change positions, not identities. I will be his nurse. I will not have the past dredged up again. I could never do that to him."

"And he has agreed to this?"

"We did not discuss it, but it will be a condition

for my staying there." She looked at him oddly. "It is very evident the ramifications that might arise should I ever be recognized. Why is that so hard for you to understand?"

He began to get scared. She was too determined, and none of it included him. "Kathryn, do you not see…I want you to marry me."

This time she did stand up, flushed and wringing her hands. "After all I have put you through?" He stood, as well, but she began to pace. "Is this because I kept throwing myself at you?"

"What are you talking about?"

"The night on the bridge, after the attack, and again after seeing all you did for my father, I literally threw myself in your arms. I assure you, you are under no obligation. Oh, dear, I am so sorry."

He stopped her and took her hands into his. "Kathryn, I feel no obligation." He lifted her chin to make her look at him. "I love you. You said you didn't think you really knew what love was nine years ago. Now I feel that way also.

"I did love you then, in a protective sort of way. I wanted to keep you safe. I wanted you always to be happy and carefree. I wanted to spoil you. Since coming to know you as Miss Montgomery *and* yourself, I realize that what I felt for you then was a fairy-tale love. Even before I knew you were you, I began to see the characteristics I want in the woman I marry. You are the embodiment of that woman."

He could see the shock on her face. Was this really such a surprise to her?

She did not pull away, but she looked at him with the saddest eyes he had seen in her yet. He knew her thoughts. "I am so sorry."

"Do not keep saying that. I thought you had grown to love me, as well."

And he saw the answer to that in the pool of tears welled up in her eyes. She *did* love him.

"That is neither here nor there." One lone tear rolled down her cheek. "I cannot marry you, my lord. If I wear the disguise to protect my father, I would feel even more honor-bound to do the same to the man I love... Marry. But I do not plan to marry. I will take care of my father, and I will try to spend as much time as I can with Jacob and Lacey as they grow up."

She did not look away. "I assure you I would have done *something* to ward this off had I known. God still torments me, and you through me. I was so happy we had come to an understanding."

"Kathryn," he said, and he was intense. He had to make her understand. "It is not God who has not forgiven you—it is *you* who has not forgiven you."

"My lord, no matter how you say it, I cannot—would never—bring any taint of scandal to you."

"What scandal?" He was running out of ways to convince her. He saw his happiness slipping away. "Even *I* did not know of it until I found you here. What would anyone else know?"

"You do not think that after nine years of least in sight, my reappearance, on *your* arm, would not have any repercussions?"

"There is only one reason I need to hear that would

keep me from marrying you. Tell me you do not love me, and I will go away and leave you in peace. Do you love me, Kathryn?"

"I love you too much to—"

"It's you!" The scream from Charity startled both of them. "Who are you? Lord Dalton, do you know this woman?" She lifted her skirt and stomped to them. "You were in our house last night. You carried Jacob out of the fire! What is going on here?" Her voice rose in intensity with each question.

Dalton finally snapped. "Charity Dinsmore!"

But he stopped as Kathryn ran away from the house, her hand covering the sobs that escaped her.

Chapter Eighteen

Dalton felt so very alone. He just wanted to be home. He needed to see his mother and hear her particular brand of wisdom.

He knew he had many friends in London and even closer relationships with the men who served with him and under him. But Kathryn completed him. It had always been that way. He had met her at an alfresco luncheon, and she was as fresh and beautiful as the whole outdoors. Indeed, she enhanced the outdoors. And he had wanted to know her from that moment.

They had been introduced by the lady hosting the luncheon, long forgotten now. When she raised her eyes to his face, he held his breath. Her eyes pulled him into her soul.

He remembered thanking God for the knowledge that He had planned this meeting before the earth was even created. Nothing had ever prepared him for the experience, and he soon learned that everything they did together from that day on *was* a new experience, whether he had done it before or not. *She* made it unique.

He never again felt comfortable without her. He accepted the wisdom of his mother, who told him not to rush his fences. He danced with others at every event so gossips would find no interest in his actions. However, he was only alive when he was with her.

Then one day she was gone. And all he could feel went with her.

And now it was happening again. He did not think he would survive it.

"Christopher!" his mother said as she entered the drawing room. "What brings you home?" She smiled at him and added, "Not that I am not delighted to see you, just surprised."

She sat before a fire, and he stooped to kiss her cheek. It almost brought him to tears.

"Christopher?" she asked warily. "What is it, son?"

She sat in a wing chair that flanked the fire and indicated he take the other. The butler brought in the tea tray and showed surprise at finding the master there. "My lord, may I pour you a glass of brandy?"

"Yes, thank you, that would be good."

When they were finally alone, his mother would not let him stay inside himself.

"Christopher, tell me what has you so blue-deviled."

"I apologize, Mother. I did not mean to be rude."

"You have not been rude, but you are completely distracted. And a little sad, I think. Do you wish to talk about it?"

"She will not have me, Mother. I have lost her again."

He had been reliving this over and over since this morning. What was the purpose of it?

"Kathryn?"

"Yes, I am sorry again. I am lost, I suppose. In order for my heart to beat again, it tells me I must have her."

"Oh, darling," she said, feeling a mother's anguish in her son's pain.

"Tell me what happened."

"I begged her to marry me, and she turned me down."

"That cannot be all there is to it, my dear. Indeed, the last time you were here, you were quite angry with her, as I recall."

"No—it sounds quite complicated, but it boils down to the fact that she is being a martyr…trying to save me pain because she fears I will suffer should her past raise its ugly head."

"So she loves you in return?"

"I believe so. She started to say it when we were interrupted by the selfish and vain daughter of Sir John. Kathryn has been particularly fearful of her because the girl is bent on figuring out who she is."

"And you do not see that as a problem?"

He finally became agitated. Maybe that is what his mother wanted. She never believed in holding things in. "No, I do not see the problem. The girl is the most recalcitrant, spoiled, out-of-control viper I have ever met. I am afraid I told her so to her face today."

His mother smiled. "Did you, dear? How positively heroic of you!"

He knew her teasing; she could pull anyone out of

the doldrums. "It was not heroic and you know it. But I will not confess it. Someone should have taken her over their knee years ago. It would have been kinder than letting her become such a termagant."

"Why is Kathryn afraid of her?"

He came back to earth with a thud. "She fears the past will haunt us if we get married. She thinks the world is full of Charitys who will stir up trouble. She cannot risk my life being ruined just by association with her."

"Are you fearful of that?"

"No, of course not. I love her. I would walk through fire for her."

"And she understands that?"

"I kept telling her."

"May I ask how you told her?"

"I do not understand."

"When she expressed her fear of such a thing happening, how did you convey your feelings on the subject?"

"I told her she was worrying for nothing. I tried to reassure her that no one could possibly find out about her past. *I* did not even know it until a few weeks ago. I told her with our connections and her father's support, no one would dare wag their tongues with questions or innuendo."

"And she fears that it is a certainty?"

"Yes, Mother." He sat down and put his head in his hands. "I cannot lose her again. I cannot."

"Son, what would happen if you did marry and the story came out?"

"What do you mean?"

"Would you rusticate until the worst blew over? Would you throw around your power as an earl and threaten a duel to the next person who spoke of your wife?"

"What an odd question! No, of course I would do none of those things. I do not care what others think. If somehow someone found that she eloped or that she had worked as a companion, what difference does it make? It was nine years ago."

"So you told her you did not care. She understood that?"

"I am not sure I used those exact words, but that is what I meant."

"Darling, what *I* heard you say is that it was too remotely possible to happen so why worry about it."

"That is correct."

She leaned over and took his hand. "My love, they are two very different things to a woman."

"I do not understand."

"You cannot convince her it will not happen—she obviously does not believe that. But if you promise her it does not matter, even if it does happen, then she has nothing to be afraid of."

"You mean…"

"Yes, I do. But it cannot be nonchalant. You need to make up your mind that you truly do not care. If you have thought about it and prayed about it and still you truly do not care if her biggest fear happens, then she does not need to save you from that."

"What have I done?"

"Nothing permanent, Christopher. Do you hear me? You were trying to convey that her worries are groundless. Her feelings and fears are real to her. But if you promise you will love her no matter what happens, then that is an entirely different matter."

He jumped up, kissing his mother's hand. "I knew I needed to be here. I knew I needed your wisdom."

"Christopher, what I am telling you still may not make her look at it any differently. But it gives her an opportunity to do what she wants instead of feeling selfish by doing it."

"Mother, would it hurt you if it ever came out in the open? I would not want to put your feelings aside for mine."

"My darling, I dare anyone to say one wrong word about my daughter-in-law. They would certainly be sorry for it."

"Thank you, Mother. I love you very much."

"Be sure and tell her that, as well!"

Kathryn sat at the base of a gnarled oak surrounded by a bed of rhododendrons and jonquils. Matty had certainly brightened her cottage since the last time she had been there. Kathryn was weeding the planted bed, but with each tug, her sadness resurfaced until Matty had to shoo her away before she started pulling up plants that belonged there.

Apologizing to her dearest friend, Kathryn moved to sit with her back against the tree for a few moments. The shade brought her relief from the heat, and she began to draw in the dirt as her mind traveled to the mess her life had become.

Kathryn had not stayed in Trotton even one night. She took the pony cart to the inn at Midhurst and had come directly to her old governess, her safe haven, as she had nine years ago and several times since.

She knew her father would be disappointed; in fact, he had told her so when he wrote back to her, but she could not hurt him again. Charity was tenacious. Kathryn knew she would not stop at discovering who she was, because she would blame her for Lord Dalton's failure to propose.

She would not lead the scandal to her father's door.

If she took this experience as a whole, she thought she might go so deeply inside of herself that she would never come out. Instead, she broke it into wedges like a pie, with each piece proving worse than the last.

Growing up, Miss Mattingly always talked about the little cottage in Uckfield that she was purchasing a tiny bit at a time with the money paid to her as Kathryn's governess. She used to tell Kathryn stories about how special it was, so small in comparison to the houses where she had been employed, but it was her special flower-bedecked retirement home where Kathryn would one day visit her with *her* children. Matty had no vision then how that small cottage would become such an oasis in every trial of Kathryn's life, beginning with her botched elopement nine years ago.

It had been her haven during the many disappointments of trying to find employment and being kicked when she was down, by mistresses who believed their husbands, sons, brothers and butlers over her. It was here in Uckfield that Matty concocted the disguise to protect her from such behavior in the future. And here she was again, lost and in pain, and she wondered how she would find the strength to start over after all that had happened to her since she ran away with Lord Salford. The only difference this time was that they would no longer be living on Matty's meager income: she had her own money now.

She brushed back what seemed an endless flow of tears. Her wonderful friend was sitting in the rocker on the little front porch tatting away, happy to be with Kathryn again, no matter the circumstances. She had often told her of God's unconditional love for her, and she believed it because that is all Matty had ever shown her. The change only came when she realized it was Matty alone who had unconditional love for her.

Enough self-pity, Kathryn thought. She wiped a stray curl off her forehead with the back of her gloved hand. "Matty, why don't I run in and get us a glass of lemonade that we may enjoy as we take a rest."

"You sit right where you are, young lady—I will get the lemonade. If it is your mission to destroy every weed in Uckfield, you will need a little fortification. I will get us a few of those scones you baked this morning, as well, and we can have a short respite while we wait for today's post. I have a feeling today will be the day God shows you the new direction He intends for you."

Kathryn only laughed at the tiny lady's forcefulness and remained seated, her back against the tree trunk behind her. She thought of the Dinsmore children once more, and memories flooded back. She had just written to them yesterday, and she sometimes wondered if Lady Dinsmore was giving her letters to them. Reflecting on their current status brought her nothing but pain. She was suddenly so very tired of it and closed her eyes, hoping to block out the dark thoughts that seemed to overtake her more often of late.

Nothing would stop Charity from trying to figure out her true identity. She could not bring scandal on her father or Lord Dalton. She could stay hidden away from the world with her only friend. Everyone else was better off without her.

She would be perfectly satisfied writing to the children and helping the poor around them. Well, nearly satisfied. At least she had memories, albeit not without blemish, but memories of Lord Dalton as he was now. She played his proposal over and over again in her mind, pretending different endings than the real one. She loved to concentrate on the moment he told her that he loved her.

She could imagine being free to return his love. She pictured a life full of laughter and a closeness she knew they would share. He would be able to take his seat in Parliament with pride, and she would support him in every way possible.

They might even have had children one day. He would be a tremendous father, his kindness making him tender and loving.

But she always awoke in the morning and remembered that none of those things were meant to be.

It was those thoughts that kept her from hearing someone enter Matty's gate and silently walk to stand before her.

"Kathryn?"

Assuming she had been dreaming, she did not immediately acknowledge his presence. It happened almost nightly since their last meeting. It was the realization that he blocked the sun from her eyes that made them open.

"Lord Dalton!"

"Kathryn, are you all right?" Matty's voice came from the front door of the little house.

"Yes, Matty. I am fine. We have a visitor." Kathryn stared at him as intently as he looked at her, but she did not move.

"I can see that. How do you do? I am Tess Mattingly."

"It is a pleasure to see you, ma'am."

"Kathryn, why don't you invite your friend to the porch and I'll bring you both that lemonade."

"Miss Mattingly, I thank you for your hospitality, but I was hoping I could talk privately with Lady Kathryn. Perhaps we might walk together? I promise I will remain out of doors and in plain sight."

"That sounds wonderful, my lord. Kathryn has been working diligently all morning. A nice walk is exactly what she needs. I will keep your lemonade to fortify you when you return."

What on earth was happening? They stood discussing her as if she was not even present. You would think they had been fast friends their whole lives!

"Lady Kathryn, will you join me?" He put his hand down to help her rise.

She did not wish to argue with him in front of her old governess, so she preceded him out of the gate. "Matty," she said over her shoulder, "we shall just walk around the duck pond. We will not be gone long."

"Take your time, dear."

They were silent at first, but he took one of her hands, entwined his fingers with hers and brought it to his lips to kiss. "It seems to me as if we have been in this position many times. Whenever I am near you, I feel the urge to hold your hand. I can even remember the first time I kissed your hand and stared into the depths of your deep blue eyes so long ago in London." He said it with a smile, and she knew he meant to put her at ease.

He released her hand. She felt bereft of it the minute the hold was broken, but she could not take it back.

"How did you find me?" She looked at him seriously and asked, "How is Father?"

"Your father is getting a little stronger all the time. But he is very sad you did not come to him when you left that day."

"You mean hurt. He is very hurt that I did not go home. It is one more hurt to be added to the list."

"He is sad, Kathryn. Just sad. He was pretty certain this is where you were. He said you mentioned the safety of Miss Mattingly's home when you went to see him."

"And he told you."

"Yes, he did. While *he* was certain, I was not. I needed to know you were all right."

"It seems you are always checking to see that I am all right."

"And it seems you are always running away, so I must be certain."

"We have been at cross-purposes for a long time."

He lost his amiability as quickly as it had come. "God's truth, Kathryn, I have so many things to say to you, I hardly know where to begin." He ran his hand through his hair. She almost smiled at the endearing gesture she now knew so well. But she could not tell him that.

"I am sorry you have come all this way to be sure of my safety, but I do appreciate it. Having both admitted our follies in the past, perhaps we may cry peace and remember the splendid friendship we began so long ago."

"No," he growled. "You know I want more. We were friends in the past, but we became more while in Trotton, did we not? Tell me we did."

"It makes no difference. I am bound by a disguise for a crime I committed in my youth. I cannot marry you. Can't you see that? Even today in the middle of nowhere, you came upon me without my disguise. If it could happen in Uckfield, it could happen anywhere." She had to choke back a sob. "There are a hundred more Charitys out there who would love to pull out the old scandal. I would make you the laughingstock of the *ton*. I will not do that to you."

"No one knows about it, Kathryn. I did not know until that night under the tree. I searched for you for weeks and found no clue!" He was getting frustrated, and she did not want them to end that way.

"Perhaps we should turn back now while we *are* still friends!" She gave him a weak smile, but he did not return it.

"I did not know about Salford until you told me about it. You were young and innocent of such blackguards. You have nothing to fear on that score. Indeed, was he not dead, I might have called him to account by now."

"Is he dead? I suspected he found another whose dowry was not tied up as mine was. I shall always be thankful for that, or I might actually be married to him." She shuddered at the thought.

"I can only imagine how scared you must have been. I felt it that night under the tree, but I was so transfixed on my own selfish feelings, I did not even attempt to comfort you." He stopped and turned to face her, putting his finger under her chin. "But you were as brave as ever. For a while I let my pride have free rein, and I blamed you for not being yourself with me. You have known for some time that is no longer the case."

She was quiet as they began to walk again, approaching the pond. She looked off in the distance. An idyllic place with the ideal man, and she could enjoy neither.

He stayed beside her, allowing her silence. But he noticed the tear roll down her cheek, and he lightly turned her to face him.

"Kathryn, I have fallen in love with you. Not the figment of my imagination on the bridge, not the disguised companion, but *you*. You are the most wonderful combination of mystery, practicality, bravery and resourcefulness I have ever seen. And I have not even touched on your wit and your ability to nurture, along with so many other things I see in you. I am making a mull of this. My pride has been in the way, but I want us to spend the rest of our lives together. I want to make up the nine years that we lost."

She pulled free and moved away from him. She began to wring her hands as the words she had once dreamed of hearing were being spoken again. Yet she knew it was impossible, and there was nothing left of her heart that had not already been broken.

"Kathryn, I want to marry you. You can decide when you are ready. If you do not wish for it now, perhaps…" He stopped as she shook her head. His voice became soft. "I love you with my whole heart and soul."

She kept shaking her head; he had begun to endow her with characteristics she did not possess. His new feelings made him forget who she really was. Well, she would remind him. "You have only known me for a few months. The first were in London when I was a child. The rest have been these past two, as a ruined woman hiding from the world out of shame.

"You say you have forgiven me, and I thank you for that—I truly do. But there are others who never will. Not the least of these being the God who forgives you. And not the rest of the world I come from." Her voice cracked, but she went on. "I am willing to continue this charade to nurse my father back to health while he can also hold his head up in Society. I was willing to give up Jacob and Lacey, but there will always be another Charity waiting to bring up the old scandal. It is better this way."

"As the daughter of a marquis who is marrying an earl, I promise you there will be no repercussions. You were too young to know about any of this when you left London. Since then you have avoided Society altogether. With such connections and with the passing of so much time, no one will care."

He held her shoulders tightly. "But in spite of your connections, and in spite of the fact that you have avoided Society—and suppose the worst should happen and someone should ask you where you have been all this time—*I...don't...care*." He emphasized the last three words.

She lowered her eyes at the intensity of his. But he would not let her. He lifted her jaw tenderly with his cupped hand. "Do you understand me? I do not care. All I care about is you."

She pulled away from him and walked toward the pond. He stayed beside her. "That is all very easy for you to say, my lord."

She heard him mumble under his breath, "She is still 'my lording' me at every turn!"

However, she continued as if she had not heard. "Yes, I avoided Society, but you have no idea of the social network that exists in the mansions and country houses of the elite. In *your* house in Town and in Rye. Servants are born into their lives, but they are not stupid. Do you think it will never come out from one of the houses where I was employed as a servant? What will your mother say when she hears your wife's name being bandied about the servant's hall?"

"First of all, my mother loves you. She always has. She knows all about this and wants this marriage almost as much as I do. But tell me, Kathryn, how would it come out? You have been in disguise at each place."

She wanted to stomp her foot as Charity did. "They are not educated as well as you and I are, but they know Kate Montgomery. They did not know Lady Kathryn because I was not in Society. Should you parade me around London on your arm, they will be able to add two and two. Then, not only will I have disappeared inexplicably nine years ago, it will be known that I have been a servant all that time. You forget, I was not always disguised."

"I am not fighting you—I just do not care."

"How can one man be so pigheaded?" This time she turned to face him. "What of Charity, my lord, and my old friends, any of whom may have had something against me? They will be spearheading the band to drum me out of the *ton*."

"They may try...I do not care."

"Very well. When all of this does come out, as it will, what will be our answer? Why did I resort to a life of servitude? What could have been so bad that I would disappear from all polite Society?" She stared at him, hard. "Only one thing—that I was ruined. Will we lie? I could—it would only be one more for me. Do you think I will let you lie? If so, you do not know me as well as you think you do."

He did not understand that this was killing her. She

wanted to say yes more than she had ever wanted anything. But she had to make him understand. She would go to any lengths, be as brutally honest as she had to be, to accomplish that. And though she did not have any heart left to break, she would die a little more inside when he was gone.

Chapter Nineteen

"Stop it!" The fear that he now understood permeated her entire being and made him want to take her into his arms and hold her, letting her struggle until it all came out. She had done that once, when he held her after her attack, but his instincts told him right now she needed the verbal reassurance that none of this mattered. He took her hand and led her to a bench under a weeping willow tree. The feathery branches just barely touched the pond, making small ripples every once in a while.

"I claim every bit as much of the responsibility for this as you do. But you have been so trampled upon, you feel that God has abandoned you. When you ran away nine years ago and I could not find you or your father, I lost sight of God, too. I lost my way. So I bought my commission in the army. I could have been of more use to my brother when my father got sick, but my pride would not let me. The consequences of that were that I did not get to say goodbye to either of them before they died. I lived through a physical hell on the Continent for four years just to keep my pride. Those were the consequences of my own bout with God. But I received His forgiveness the moment I asked for it. And I believe I am the man I am today because God used that part of my life for good."

He watched the tears roll silently down her cheeks. "Do you want me to stop?"

She shook her head.

"You made a mistake. It was no worse than others have made. Did you seek God? Did you ask Him for forgiveness, Kathryn?"

"Of course I did. I searched for Him with all my heart. But every prayer was answered with no."

He grabbed her hands. "Not with no, but with wait. There were consequences to your mistake, but would you ever have touched the lives of those two children, or would they have touched yours, without those consequences? Do you know that when we were in London, I used to tell my mother you were my fragile flower? I never wanted you to know one hardship in your life. I was going to protect you from everything.

"Do you even realize the woman you have become? You are so amazing and strong, yet loving and giving and so much more. I might have smothered you to death had we married then. But Kathryn, you were forgiven the first moment you asked for it."

She broke his gaze and looked over toward the pond. His heart sank; he had not reached her.

And he did not know what else to say.

Finally she turned back to him, but her eyes were steely blue. She had hardened her heart again. "And that I am ruined, my lord, is that no longer of any importance to you?"

"No it is not." He took hold of her hands and knelt down before her. "I made a hasty judgment that night. But I have no right to judge anyone, and certainly no right to judge you. I am more sorry than I can say about that. I took the hurt I felt and turned it on you in the worst way. I took a horrible part of your life and threw it in your face. I *let* you relive the shame you place on yourself. I did that.

"I know the reason I did it. I did not want to appear as anything less than the confident, righteous earl, but the only part that has ever really bothered me is that you chose someone over me. I did not ask you why you eloped that night. If I had, I would have learned what I learned in the carriage two weeks ago. That's when I learned it was really all my fault. But I let you feel shame at a youthful indiscretion.

"Do you still believe I am the kindest man you know?" He put his head in her lap. "Can you forgive me?"

He was desperate; he could feel her slipping away, and he could not lose her again.

"Kathryn?"

"I am sorry, my lord. I think we have said all there is to say."

No! They could not have come so far for this. He raised his head, took her hands in his and said, "We can do this, my darling. We can hold our heads high no matter what comes our way, and we will get through it and give the glory to God. We will have our entire lives to heal from some of these wounds, but we must do it together. If we give up now, it will all have been wasted."

She could not resist the urge to touch him. She stroked his hair as she would a brokenhearted child. Was his heart broken as hers was? Was he really ready to risk the condemnation of everything he had ever known for *her?*

Lord, I do not know what to pray. I do not know what to do. My father always told me if I felt far from You, it was me who moved, not You. I am taking my first step back to You now. Please show me what to do.

Dalton lifted his head from her lap and sat down on the ground at her feet, his back up against the bench. He faced the pond and they sat quietly, both wondering what to do next. Had she been silly asking God to give her a sign? Even far away from Him, she knew He rarely worked that way.

"Kathryn, I need to confess something I've done before you hear it from someone else. I promise you, I thought only of you. I saw a way I thought would make you happy, make all of this easier on you."

"Pray tell me."

"You may not have noticed in the shock of seeing me, but I have corresponded several times with Miss Mattingly."

"I do not understand."

"When your father told me that this was probably where you were, I wrote to her to discover if that was so and to find out about your well-being. I know it was presumptuous of me, but I was worried. And I missed you."

Still he sat looking straight ahead. "When she confirmed you were with her, I asked her if I could come see you. I told her I wanted to pick up Lacey and Jacob and bring them for a visit. I wanted to surprise you."

"What?" She was amazed, more than amazed, though she knew she should not be. His thoughtfulness had always been one of the things she loved most about him.

"She loves you very much. She told me she thought you needed a little more time to put things into perspective in your own mind. Of course she knew about your love for those children, but she could not be sure whether a visit from them would make you happy or leave you brokenhearted again." He was quiet. "She is a very wise woman."

"A great deal wiser than me," she responded. "When you first said it, I wished you *had* brought them. But I know myself. It would have been too hard to say goodbye again, not knowing when I would see them or if they were being taken care of properly."

She could imagine his impatience, waiting for the responses from Matty before every decision. He listened to Matty, he agreed to give her, as well as the children, some healing time together.

Now she did not know if she *could* throw that kind of love away.

He spoke again. "I thought I heard something in her words that I could not be sure of in a letter. So one day, while you were visiting neighbors, I visited your Miss Mattingly."

"I cannot believe this! To what purpose, my lord?" She was not angry, but confused, and a little hurt.

"To offer her the position as Lacey and Jacob's governess."

She was speechless! She tried to rise, but her legs got tangled in his boots, and she literally fell into his lap. She was a bit stunned, but she looked at him and saw his smile, accompanied by those mesmerizing dimples. They both laughed at the predicament she now found herself in. Their eyes locked, and she saw nothing but love gazing back at her. It would be so easy to stay there, but she soon returned to her senses and tried to get up.

"Can we not finish our discussion here?" he asked. "You would not wish to get your frock dirty sitting on the ground, and I know you would never stand over me, glaring like one of my old tutors."

"You are trying to change the subject," she said, forgetting all about her indelicate location on his lap. "What right did *you* have to offer Matty a position in the Dinsmore household? Indeed, why would you offer her a position at all? Now that I am here, Matty has no need to support herself."

"Which of those items would you like me to address first?"

"All of them!"

He laughed out loud and hugged her to him. "Very well. I will answer them in the correct order. I thought I gleaned from one of her letters that she missed the relationships with children that being a governess afforded her. She knew she would love Lacey and Jacob because you do. I came to see her because I *needed* to know about you. Not seeing you was too hard."

She blushed, and for once did not object.

"She assured me you were well physically, but she thought you were struggling emotionally. One of those issues was Jacob and Lacey. So I asked her if I had been correct in thinking she was not sure she wished to retire yet. She admitted that when you spoke of them, she began to worry about them, as well. If she could find special children like that, she thought she would enjoy watching one more generation of little ones grow up."

"Why did she never tell me this?"

"I do not think it was something that weighed on her mind. I was asking her questions that led to the answer I sought." She knew she should remove herself from his lap, but each time she thought about it, he went on with his story and she did not want to miss a thing.

"When I left here, I went to see Lady Dinsmore in London."

At that, she turned to face him. They were only inches apart. "You *have* been busy!"

He continued immediately. "I told her we always had the children on our minds. Believe it or not, I have come to love them, too, you know. Once I looked at them through your eyes, it was impossible not to." She lowered her eyes; they were so close and he stared at her so intently.

"The lady admitted they were quite changed since you were gone."

"Oh, no!"

"She thought they were not as exuberant in their lessons and free time. I asked her if she was looking for a governess. She told me she knew they needed one, but she could never replace you."

Tears fell down her cheeks.

"I told her I might know of someone, and I could let her know should that special person be available."

She trembled a little as he touched his forehead to hers. "Do not cry, love. When I left London, I decided I needed to see them for myself. I knew you would expect a firsthand report!" He smiled again. "They are fine, though I had to answer a thousand questions about you. 'Who does Miss Montgomery take with her on her learning days?' 'Is Miss Montgomery still working on her sampler for the nursery?' 'Tell Miss Montgomery the nursery only smells a little of smoke now.' You are loved as much as you love them."

She actually smiled at that, and reached a hand up to his face. "Thank you."

"You are very welcome."

Lord, my heart is changing. He is so loving. Could You be showing me this?

"I wrote to Miss Mattingly and asked if she would like the position. Obviously, it would depend on an agreement between both participants, but would she even consider it? I promised neither of the ladies anything, and I did not give Lady Dinsmore Miss Mattingly's name."

Kathryn's head shot up. "Has Matty agreed?" She threw her arms around his neck, and feelings of joy overflowed. *God, this must be You!* Was he really willing to risk everything to please her? Would he take on the entire upper ten thousand of the *ton?*

"She has not said yes yet. As you are well aware, you mean more to her than anyone else on this earth. This is not to make you feel guilty, but she would not give it a thought while you needed her. And she will talk about this with you when you are alone. The two of you will make the decision together."

She removed her arms from his shoulders. "I am the linchpin upon which all else turns?"

"You are the biggest part, but that is because we all love you so much. You are first in our hearts. Miss Mattingly will take the position for her own sake, and to take your worry about those children off your shoulders. You are free to live here for as long as you like, if that is your wish. Your father wants you home with him very badly. If Miss Mattingly takes the position, you have a place with him, and you would not be far from the children."

"But Charity…she will find out the truth, and the scandal will reach him."

"Love, you must forget about Charity. Let go of that fear. The only thing she knows about you, or will ever know about you, is that you were her companion. Highborn ladies with no fortune take such positions often— more shame on us. *If* she takes the time to worry over it, no one will listen to her—but more importantly, there is nothing in her brainbox but herself. She will forget about you the day she walks into a London modiste."

"You speak in jest, but the threat remains."

"I speak the truth. But I do not wish to waste any

more time discussing Charity Dinsmore. I want to give you a third option."

Kathryn tensed. She knew what was coming.

"You can marry me. Miss Mattingly will be happy with Jacob and Lacey, and they with her. We can stay at your father's whenever you wish, for as long as you wish. I know you will feel better nursing him yourself.

"You do love me, Kathryn. Please say it."

Father, instead of giving me the way to go, You have given me many! Can the past really be in the past? I said I would trust You....

"Yes, my lord, I do love you."

She let him put her arms around his neck once more. He slowly lowered her back just a bit and leaned in to place a tender kiss on her lips. She had waited six and twenty years for her first kiss, and it was the most natural thing in the world to tighten her arms a little and return it tenderly, trying to convey how powerful his love was to her. She felt nine years of pain and confusion fall off her shoulders, to be replaced with perfect peace.

"Will you marry me, my one and only love?" he asked as he kissed her again. "Say yes," he said, kissing her one more time before she smiled at him with loving sapphire eyes.

"Yes, my love, I will marry you."

He held her so tightly she could scarce breathe, but she did not care. After a moment she pulled away, but just a little.

"Christopher?"

"Yes, my fairy?"

It made her smile to remember that first night on the Rother River Bridge. But she must get her point across.

"When we are walking down Bond Street and we run into Charity Dinsmore, do you still think she will forget all about me?"

He groaned and ran his hand through his hair. This time she could not hide her smile.

"I think she will remember you, indeed, and I pray it is with the understanding that I *always* preferred the beauty in disguise."

* * * * *

If you enjoyed this story by Mary Moore,
be sure to check out the rest of the
Love Inspired Historical books this month!

Dear Reader,

I hope you enjoyed reading about the journey of Kathryn and Dalton. I can tell you that they took me on quite a journey!

From the beginning, I had a story and a message I wanted you to be able to relate to, encased in a sweet romance. But that story fought back at every turn. I couldn't make the characters fit into the significance of the message without bogging down the romance. Or the romance didn't work when I tried to squeeze it into the message. It was then I realized that I was trying to put my message and my characters into a story that belonged to God!

At that point, I turned the story and the characters over to Him. I wanted His message to be paramount, not mine. So I asked for His forgiveness, and with that, He gave me new insight, a new direction and the message that He had just taught me. With *Ephesians* 4:32 as the theme, "And be kind to one another, tender-hearted, forgiving each other, just as God in Christ also has forgiven you," the sweet love story became more of a struggle between Kathryn and Dalton, but maybe ended even sweeter because of the greater effort that was required of them to find that love.

I pray that you found something to touch your heart in this story. If so, I give all of the glory to God. Thank you for taking the time to read *Beauty In Disguise.* I would love to hear from you. Please visit my website, www.marymooreauthor.com, and drop me a note.

God bless you,
Mary

Questions for Discussion

1. From the beginning of the book, we were introduced to two women, Kathryn and Charity. One was beautiful on the inside, and one was beautiful on the outside. Do you think society today is as concerned with working on inner beauty as much as outer beauty?

2. What characteristics did Kathryn display as Miss Montgomery that made her so likeable despite her appearance?

3. Haven't we all made the mistake of judging someone based on their appearance? Or have we judged someone based on their circumstances? Can you think of an instance where that has been brought home to you?

4. Regency London had strict codes of conduct. Kathryn believed she deserved to be ostracized for eloping. She thought herself unworthy of forgiveness. Are there things in your life you haven't forgiven yourself for?

5. Kathryn even believed that God had forsaken her. Do you think He denies His forgiveness if we ask for it? Have you ever experienced that kind of hurt, either personally or in someone you know?

6. Kathryn and Dalton were apart for nine years, knowing nothing of the other's situation. Once they meet again, they believe too much time has passed for them to "forgive and forget." Is it ever too late to forgive someone? Have you had an experience with a lack of forgiveness either on your part or that of someone else?

7. When Kathryn ran away, she felt the need to deceive the people she came into contact with by wearing a disguise. The deception was used for different purposes, but does the end justify the means?

8. Both Kathryn and Dalton literally ran away from their problems. Have you ever run away from a problem by avoiding certain people or places because of the expectation of what might happen?

9. Did you become emotionally attached to any one character in the story? Why?

10. Kathryn was blessed to have a relationship with a sincere, godly woman in Miss Mattingly. What is the importance of having the fellowship and advice of such friends during the hard times of your life?

11. All three of the Dinsmore children were flawed, either to the point of being spoiled, or the opposite— starving for affection. How great is the importance

of the influence our parents have on our character and overall lives? Share an experience in your own life.

12. Kathryn and Dalton had wonderful, playful senses of humor. Is that something you identified with? Do you use it in your own relationship with others?

13. Forgiveness and beauty that is only skin deep are themes throughout the story. What other themes stood out for you? Why?

14. What did you think of the Regency setting as the background for the story? Would you read more stories set in that time period? Why?

15. Discuss one or two of your favorite things about this book, and discuss one or two of your least favorite things.

REQUEST YOUR FREE BOOKS!

2 FREE INSPIRATIONAL NOVELS
PLUS 2
FREE
MYSTERY GIFTS

Love Inspired.

HISTORICAL

INSPIRATIONAL HISTORICAL ROMANCE

YES! Please send me 2 FREE Love Inspired® Historical novels and my 2 FREE mystery gifts (gifts are worth about $10). After receiving them, if I don't wish to receive any more books, I can return the shipping statement marked "cancel." If I don't cancel, I will receive 4 brand-new novels every month and be billed just $4.49 per book in the U.S. or $4.99 per book in Canada. That's a saving of at least 22% off the cover price. It's quite a bargain! Shipping and handling is just 50¢ per book in the U.S. and 75¢ per book in Canada.* I understand that accepting the 2 free books and gifts places me under no obligation to buy anything. I can always return a shipment and cancel at any time. Even if I never buy another book, the two free books and gifts are mine to keep forever.

102/302 IDN FVXK

Name	(PLEASE PRINT)	

Address		Apt. #

City	State/Prov.	Zip/Postal Code

Signature (if under 18, a parent or guardian must sign)

Mail to the Harlequin® Reader Service:
IN U.S.A.: P.O. Box 1867, Buffalo, NY 14240-1867
IN CANADA: P.O. Box 609, Fort Erie, Ontario L2A 5X3

Want to try two free books from another series?
Call 1-800-873-8635 or visit www.ReaderService.com.

* Terms and prices subject to change without notice. Prices do not include applicable taxes. Sales tax applicable in N.Y. Canadian residents will be charged applicable taxes. Offer not valid in Quebec. This offer is limited to one order per household. Not valid for current subscribers to Love Inspired Historical books. All orders subject to credit approval. Credit or debit balances in a customer's account(s) may be offset by any other outstanding balance owed by or to the customer. Please allow 4 to 6 weeks for delivery. Offer available while quantities last.

Your Privacy—The Harlequin® Reader Service is committed to protecting your privacy. Our Privacy Policy is available online at www.ReaderService.com or upon request from the Harlequin Reader Service.

We make a portion of our mailing list available to reputable third parties that offer products we believe may interest you. If you prefer that we not exchange your name with third parties, or if you wish to clarify or modify your communication preferences, please visit us at www.ReaderService.com/consumerschoice or write to us at Harlequin Reader Service Preference Service, P.O. Box 9062, Buffalo, NY 14269. Include your complete name and address.

LIH13

The wrong groom could be the
perfect match in

GROOM BY ARRANGEMENT

by **Rhonda Gibson**

Eliza Kelly thought her humiliation was complete when she
identified the wrong train passenger as her mail-order groom.
She was only trying to tell Jackson Hart that the madcap scheme
was *not* her idea. When the blacksmith decides to stay, he offers
the lovely widow a marriage of convenience. Between caring for
an orphaned youngster and protecting Eliza, Jackson feels whole
again. If only he can persuade Eliza to marry him, and fulfill
their long-buried dreams of forging a real family.

Available in February wherever books are sold.

All Laura White wants is a second chance.
Will she find it in Cooper Creek?

Read on for a preview of
THE COWBOY'S HEALING WAYS.

The door opened, bringing in cool air and a few stray drops of rain. The man in the doorway slipped off boots and hung a cowboy hat on a hook by the door. She watched as he shrugged out of his jacket and hung it next to his hat.

When he turned, she stared up at a man with dark hair that brushed his collar and lean, handsome features. He looked as at home in this big house as he did in his worn jeans and flannel shirt. His dark eyes studied her with curious suspicion. She'd gotten used to that look. She'd gotten used to people whispering behind their hands as she walked past.

But second chances and starting over meant wanting something new. She wanted to be the person people welcomed into their lives. She wanted to be the woman a man took a second look at, maybe a third.

Jesse Cooper took a second look, but it was a look of suspicion.

"Jesse, I'm so glad you're here." Granny Myrna had returned with a cold washcloth, which she placed on Laura's forehead. "It seems I had an accident."

"Really?" Jesse smiled a little, warming the coolness in dark eyes that focused on Laura.

"I pulled right out in front of her. She drove her car off the side of the road to keep from hitting me."

Laura closed her eyes. A cool hand touched the gash at her hairline.

"Let me see this."

She opened her eyes and he was squatting in front of her, studying the cut. He looked from the gash to her face. Then he moved and stood back up, unfolding his long legs with graceful ease. Laura clasped her hands to keep them from shaking.

A while back there had been an earthquake in Oklahoma. Laura remembered when it happened, and how they'd all wondered if they'd really felt the earth move or if it had been their imaginations. She was pretty sure it had just happened again. The earth had moved, shifting precariously as a hand touched her face and dark eyes studied her intently, with a strange mixture of curiosity, surprise and something else.

*Will Jesse ever allow the mysterious Laura
into his life—and his heart?*

*Pick up THE COWBOY'S HEALING WAYS
by Brenda Minton,
available in February 2013 from Love Inspired.*

Sweetheart Bride

by *New York Times* bestselling author

Lenora Worth

Restoring not just a house but a heart, as well

When architect Nick Santiago recruits Brenna Blanchard to help restore a beautiful old mansion, it's just the distraction she needs from her recent broken wedding engagement— and growing close to handsome Nick is an unexpected bonus. Except, Nick is all business. Can Brenna help him arrange his priorities—with love as number one?

Available February 2013!